Indulge in some perfect romance
from the incomparable

PENNY JORDAN

The all new Penny Jordan
large print collection gives you
your favourite glamorous
Penny Jordan stories in
easier-to-read print.

THE
ITALIAN DUKE'S
VIRGIN MISTRESS

Penny Jordan

First published in Great Britain 2010
by Mills & Boon, an imprint of Harlequin (UK) Limited.
Large Print edition 2011
Harlequin (UK) Limited,
Eton House, 18-24 Paradise Road,
Richmond, Surrey TW9 1SR

© Penny Jordan 2010

ISBN: 978 0 263 22960 8

Harlequin (UK) policy is to use papers that are natural,
renewable and recyclable products and made from
wood grown in sustainable forests. The logging and
manufacturing process conform to the legal environmental
regulations of the country of origin.

Printed and bound in Great Britain
by CPI Antony Rowe, Chippenham, Wiltshire

CHAPTER ONE

'ARE you Charlotte Wareham, the project manager from Kentham Brothers?'

Charlotte—Charley—Wareham looked up from her laptop, blinking in the strong Italian spring sunshine. She had only just returned from a snatched, very late lunch—a sandwich and a cup of delicious cappuccino in a local café. Her meeting with the two civic dignitaries responsible for the restoration project on a derelict public garden, to be completed for the five hundredth anniversary of the garden's creation, which she would be overseeing, had overrun badly.

The man now towering over her, whom she hadn't met before, and who seemed to have appeared out of nowhere, was plainly angry—

very angry indeed—as he gestured towards the cheap faux stone urns and other replica samples she had shipped over for client inspection.

'And what, may I ask, are these vile abominations?' he demanded.

It wasn't his anger, though, that had a coil of shocked disbelief tightening her whole body. Dimly she recognised that the sharp, swift pang of sensation possessing her was instinctive female recognition of a man so alpha that no woman could or would even want to deny him.

This was a man born to stand head and shoulders above his peers—a man born to produce strong sons in his own image—a man born to take the woman of his choice to his bed and to give her such pleasure there that she would be bound to him by the mere memory for the rest of her life.

She must have been sitting in the sun for too long, Charley decided shakily. Such thoughts were certainly not something she was normally prone to—quite the opposite.

She made a determined effort to pull herself

together, putting her laptop down, rising from the faux stone bench on which she had been sitting, and standing up to confront her interrogator.

He was tall and dark and as filled with furious rage as a volcano about to erupt. He was also, as her senses had already recognised, extraordinarily good-looking. His olive-toned skin was drawn smoothly over the tautly masculine bone structure of his face, and he was tall, dark-haired, with the kind of arrogantly proud chiselled features that spoke of patrician forebears. His unexpectedly steely grey-eyed gaze swept over her with open contempt, his look like a sculptor's chisel, seeking the exact spot in a piece of marble where it was most vulnerable.

Charley tried to look away from him and found instead that her gaze had somehow slipped to his mouth. Shocked by her own behaviour, she tried to drag her gaze away, but it refused to move. Prickles of warning quivered over her skin, but it was already too late. An unwanted jolt of awareness of him as a man had already struck through her like forked lightning coming out of a still, calm sky, and was all the more frightening for that unexpectedness. Her mouth had gone dry; a thousand tiny nerve-endings were pulsing beneath her skin. She could feel her lips softening and swelling as though in preparation for a lover's kiss, and he was looking at them now, his gaze narrowed and unreadable, but no doubt filled with arrogant disdain for her weakness. A man like this one would never look at her mouth the way she had looked at his. He would never be caught off guard by the sudden shock of knowing that his senses had torn free of his mind and were imagining what it would be like to feel her mouth against his.

Jerkily, her fingers trembling as she fought for self-control, Charley pulled down the sunglasses perched on top of her head to cover her eyes, in an attempt to conceal the effect he was having on her. But it was too late. He had seen it—and the contempt she could see hardening his expression told her what he thought of her reaction to him. Her face, her whole body was burning with a mixture of shocked disbelief and humiliation as she battled to rationalise and understand what had happened to her. She simply didn't *ever* react to men like that, and it shocked her that she had done so now—and to this man of all men. She had an unnerving need to touch her own lips, to see if they actually were as softly swollen as they felt.

What had happened must be some kind of reaction to all the pressure and stress she had been under, Charley tried to rationalise. Why else would she be reacting in this uncharacteristic and dangerous way? Her senses, though, refused to be controlled. The artist's eye within her recognised the raw male power of the body that was cloaked by his undoubtedly expensive charcoal-grey suit. Beneath his clothes he would have the kind of torso, and everything that went with it, that the medieval artists for which

Florence was so justly famous had so loved to sculpt and paint.

Too late she recognised that he was still waiting for her to respond to his question. In a bid to regain the ground she felt she had lost, Charley lifted her small pointed chin and told him, 'I do work for Kentham Brothers, yes.' She paused, trying not to wince as she looked at the haphazard line of pots and statues, their shoddiness laid bare by the stranger's disdain, and then continued, 'And the "vile abominations", as you call them, are in fact very good value for money.'

The look of contempt that twisted his mouth into bitter cynicism—not just at the samples but also at her—confirmed everything Charley already knew about herself. The truth was that she was as lacking in true beauty, style and elegance, and every other female attribute there was that a man might admire as the samples were lacking in anything truly artistic. And it was that knowledge—the knowledge that she had been judged and found wanting by a man who was no doubt a true connoisseur of her sex—that prompted her to tell him defiantly, 'Not that it is really any of your business...' She paused deliberately before adding a questioning, 'Signor...?'

The dark eyebrows snapped towards the bridge of his arrogant, aquiline nose, the grey eyes turning molten platinum as he gave her an arrogantly lofty look and told her, 'It is not Signor anything, Ms Wareham. I am Raphael Della Striozzi—Duce di Raverno. Il Duce is the form of address most people of the town use to address me—as they have addressed my father and his father before him, going back for many centuries.'

Il Duce? He was a duke? Well, she wasn't going to let herself be impressed, Charley told herself, especially since he was obviously expecting her to be.

'Really?' Charley stuck her chin out determinedly—a habit she had developed as a child, to defend herself from parental criticism. 'Well, I should point out to you that this whole area is strictly off-limits to the general public, titled or untitled, for their own safety. There are notices in place. If you have issues with the restoration work which Kentham Brothers has been commissioned to do, I suggest that you take them up with the authorities,' she told him briskly.

Raphael stared at her in furious disbelief. She, this Englishwoman, was *daring* to attempt to deny him access to this garden?

'I am not the general public. It was a member of my family who originally bequeathed this garden to the town.'

'Yes, I know that,' Charley agreed. She had done her research on the garden very thoroughly when she had first been told about the contract. 'The garden was a gift to the townspeople from the wife of the first duke, in thanks to them for praying for the birth of a son after four daughters.'

Raphael's mouth hardened into a grim line, as he returned, 'Thank you, I am well aware of the history of my family.'

But it was only when he had looked into the matter more thoroughly that he had discovered the ornamentation this woman intended to replace with hideous examples of modern mass production had originally been created by some of the Renaissance's most gifted artists. Now abandoned, damaged and forgotten, the garden had been designed by a foremost landscaper of the day.

The realisation of how magnificent the garden must have been had stirred within him a sense of responsibility towards the current project. A responsibility he should have been aware of earlier, and which he now blamed himself for not shouldering before. The town might own the garden, but they carried the name of his family, and next year, when it was reopened to the public in celebration of its five hundredth year of existence, that connection was bound to be publicly referred to. Raphael took pride in the proper artistic maintenance of all the historic buildings and art treasures that had come down to him through his family, and the thought of the garden to which his family was connected being given a makeover more suited to an English suburban plot owned by people with dubious taste filled him with an anger that was currently directed towards Charlotte Wareham—with her make-up-less face, her sun-streaked mud-brown hair, and her obvious lack of interest or pride in her appearance. She was as ill equipped to match the fabled beauty of her renaissance peers as her revolting statues were of matching the magnificence of the originals that had once graced this garden.

He looked again at Charley, frowning as a second look forced him to revise his earlier assessment of her. Now he could see that her pink, lipstick-free mouth was soft, her lips full and well shaped, her nose and jaw delicately sculpted. He had initially thought her eyes, with their thick dark lashes, above cheekbones currently stained with angry colour, a light plain blue, but now, with her anger aroused, he could see they had become the extraordinarily brilliant blue-green of the Adriatic at its most turbulent.

It didn't matter what she looked like, Raphael told himself grimly.

Charley could feel her face starting to burn with memories of her parents warning her about thinking before she spoke or acted, and the un-feminine hastiness of her desire to answer back when challenged. She had believed that she had learned to control that aspect of her person-ality, but this man—this…this duke—had somehow or other managed to get under her skin and prove her wrong. Now she felt as though he had wrong-footed her, but she wasn't going to let him see that.

'Well, you may be the Duke of Raverno, but it says nothing in the paperwork I have seen about a duke having any involvement in this project. As I understand it, no matter what part your ancestors may have played in the garden in the past, it is the town that is now respon-sible for them and their restoration. You have no right to be here.'

She wasn't going to let him bully her, not for one minute—title or no title. She had had enough of that over these last few weeks, with her employer making her life such a misery that she longed to be able to hand in her notice. But she had to grin and bear it in the current financial climate. Her small household, which included her elder sister, her younger sister and her twin sons, desperately needed the money she earned—all the more so since her elder sister's interior design business was on the verge of collapse.

With so many people unemployed, she was lucky just to have a job—something her employer continually pointed out to her. She knew why he was doing that, of course. Times were hard; he wanted to cut back on his staff, and he had a daughter fresh out of university, working as an intern within the business, who'd thrown a complete hissy fit when she'd learned that Charley was going to be overseeing this new Italian contract.

If it hadn't been for the fact that she spoke

Italian, and her boss's daughter did not, Charley knew she would already have lost her job. She would probably lose it anyway once this contract had been completed. So, she might have to let her employer treat her appallingly, because she desperately needed to keep her job, but she wasn't going to let this arrogant Italian do the same thing. Not when it was the town council she was answerable to and not him. And besides, challenging him made her feel much better about her unwanted awareness of him.

Raphael could feel the fury building up inside him—burning and boiling inside him like molten lava.

When the town council had announced that they planned to restore the dangerously dilapidated pleasure garden just outside the town walls, he had instituted a search of the ducal archives for copies of the original plans for the garden, initially simply out of curiosity, thinking they might assist with the renovation. However, when he had returned from Rome to discover that for financial reasons the town had decided to replace the statues and other features originally designed and created by some of Florence's greatest renaissance artists he had been appalled—and his temper had been left on edge by the council's assertion that the garden would either have to be restored within the small budget available or the site completely flattened, because in its present state it constituted a danger to the public. And now here was this Englishwoman, whose challenge to him was igniting his fury to near uncontrollable levels.

Raphael might not welcome what was planned for the restoration of the garden, but he welcomed even less the effect this young woman responsible for managing the restoration was having on him. Such was the intensity of his anger that it was fostering within him a desire to punish her for daring to provoke it in him. And that could not be allowed. Not now or ever.

Anger and cruelty were the twin demons that

together created men whose savage legacy could never be forgotten or forgiven. And the propensity to exhibit them flowed as surely through his veins as it had done through the ancestors who had passed down that legacy to him—but with him that inheritance would end. He had vowed that as a thirteen-year-old, watching as his mother's coffin was placed in the family vault in Rome to join that of his father.

Raphael looked unseeingly towards the padlocked entrance to the gardens. He could feel the heavy, threatening shadow of those twin emotions at his back, following him, out of sight but always there, over his shoulder…

They ran through his family like a dark curse, waiting to escape. He had taught himself to imprison them with reason and ethical awareness, to deny them the arrogance and pride that were their life blood, but now, out of nowhere, simply by being here this Englishwoman had brought him to such a pitch of fierce passion, with her tawdry, ugly replicas, her lack of awareness of what the garden should be, that the key to freeing them was now in the lock without him even being aware of putting it there. Forcing back his urge to physically take hold of her and force her to study the original plans of the garden, to see the damage she would be doing to such a historical asset, was like trying to stem a river in full flood, straining every emotional and mental sinew he had.

The walls of his self-control had already been tested by his meeting with the town council as he had studied the plans they had so proudly showed him, while telling him what a bargain they had secured. And now here was this…this woman, so slender that he could have broken her with his bare hands, daring to deny him access to the garden his ancestor had originally created, expecting him to accept the shoddy, tawdry mockery of the artistic elegance and beauty that had once been.

'You have no right…' she had said. Well, he would *make* it his right—he would make the garden what it should be, and he would make her…

Make her what? A sacrifice to the darkness within his genes?

No! Never that. Nothing and no one would be allowed to threaten his control over that dark, dangerous capacity for savagely violent anger that ran through his veins and was patterned in his DNA.

He needed to speak to the local authorities and put before them the plan he was now formulating—for *him* to take control of the restoration project, so that it could be placed in more appropriate hands, and the sooner the better.

Unaware of what Raphael was thinking, Charley was both surprised and relieved when he started to stride away from her, moving to climb into a sleek, expensive-looking car parked several yards away, its bodywork the same steel-grey colour as his eyes.

CHAPTER TWO

CHARLEY looked worriedly at her watch. Where was the haulier the town officials had assured her would arrive to collect the supplier's samples? In another fifteen minutes the taxi booked to take her to the airport in Florence would be here, and Charley was far too conscientious to simply get into it without ensuring the samples were safely on their way back to the suppliers. She was beginning to wish now that she had spoken with the carriers herself, instead of accepting the city official's offer to do so for her.

Her earlier run-in with 'The Duke' had left her feeling far more unsettled and on edge than she wanted to admit. It had been a long couple of days, filled with meetings and site inspections, and the realisation of the enormity of the task of restoring the garden. Privately, it had saddened her to examine the overgrown, broken-down site and recognise how beautiful it must once have been, knowing that the budget they had been given could not possibly allow them to return it to anything like its former glory. And now, instead of being able to indulge in a few days of relaxing in Florence, soaking up everything it had to offer, she had to fly straight back to Manchester because there was no way her boss would allow her any time off. Not that she could have afforded to stay in Florence, even if he had been willing to let her take some leave. Every penny was precious in their small household, and Charley wasn't about to waste money on herself when they were struggling just to keep a roof over their heads.

A van came round the corner of the dusty road and pulled up virtually alongside her with a screech of tyres. The doors of the van were thrown open and two young men got out, one of them going to the rear of the vehicle to open the doors and the other heading for the samples.

This was the freight authority that had been organised? Charley watched anxiously, her anxiety turning to dismay when she saw the rough manner in which the young men were handling the samples.

But worse was to come. When they reached the open rear doors of the van, to Charley's disbelief they simply threw two of the samples into it, causing both of them to break.

'Stop it! Stop what you are doing,' Charley demanded in Italian, rushing to stand in front of the remaining samples.

'We have orders to remove this rubbish,' one of them told her, his manner polite, but quite obviously determined.

'Orders? Who from?'

'Il Duce,' he answered, edging past her to pick up another of the samples.

Il Duce! How dared he? Hard on the heels of her outraged anger came the knowledge that she must stop them—or face the wrath of both the supplier who had entrusted the samples to her and her employer.

'No. You can't do this. You must stop,' Charley protested frantically. There was close on a thousand pounds' worth of goods here, and the damage would be laid at her door. Out of the corner of her eye she saw a familiar grey car speed towards them, throwing up clouds of dust as its driver brought it to a halt on the roadside several yards away and then got out.

As soon as he was within earshot, Charley demanded, 'What's going on? Why are these men destroying the samples? The damage will have to be paid for, and—'

'They are acting on my orders, since I am now in charge of the restoration project, and it is my wish that they are disposed of.'

He was now in charge? It was *his* wish that they were disposed of? And would it also be his wish that she was disposed of—or rather that her services were dispensed with? Did she really need to ask herself that question?

Helplessly Charley watched as the final sample was loaded into the van.

'Where are they taking them? What you're doing is theft, you know.' She tried valiantly to protect the supplier's goods, but The Duke didn't deign to answer her, going to speak to the two young men instead. Charley looked at her watch again. She could do nothing about the samples now. But where was her taxi? If it didn't arrive soon not only would she be responsible for the loss of the samples, she would also miss her flight. She could just imagine how her boss was going to react. Only her fluency in Italian had prevented him from sacking her already, so that he could give his daughter her job.

She reached into her bag for her mobile. She would have to ring the council official who had organised the taxi for her.

The white van was speeding away, and The Duke had come back to her.

'There are matters we need to discuss,' he told her peremptorily.

'I'm waiting for a taxi to pick me up and take me to the airport.'

'The taxi has been cancelled.'

Cancelled? Charley was feeling sick with anxiety now, but she wasn't going to let it show—not to this man of all men.

'Follow me,' he commanded.

Follow him? Charley opened her mouth to object, and then closed it again as out of nowhere the knowledge came to her that this was a man who had the power to make a woman lose so much sense of herself that following him would be all she wanted to do. But not her, Charley assured herself—and yet wasn't that exactly what she was doing? Something about him compelled her to obey him, to follow him, as though…as though she was commanded by something outside her own rational control. Her whole body shuddered as immediately and physically as though he had actually touched her, and had found a reaction to that touch that she herself had not wanted to give. What was she *thinking*?

He was striding towards the car, leaving her with no option than to do as he had instructed her. He was opening the passenger door of the car for her.

He was taking her to the airport? And what had he meant when he had said that he was taking over the project?

She could all too easily picture him in Florence at the time of the Medicis, manipulating politics to suit his own purposes, with the aid of his sword if necessary, claiming whatever he wanted, be it wealth or a woman, and making it his possession. He had that air of darkness and danger about him. She shivered again, but this time not with angry resentment. This time the frisson of sensation that stroked her body was making her aware of him as a man, unnerving and alarming her.

He was not someone who would have any compassion for those weaker than him—especially if they were in his way, or if he had marked them out as his prey, Charley warned herself. Let him do his worst—think the worst of her. She didn't care. She had far more important things to worry about, like keeping her job and keeping her all-important salary flowing into the family bank account; like doing her bit and following the example of selfless sacrifice her elder sister Lizzie had set. Her sister always managed to make light of all that she had done for them, never revealing that she felt any hint of the shameful misery that Charley sometimes had to fight off because she had been forced to give up her private dreams of working in the world of fine art. Sometimes Charley admitted she felt desperately constricted, her artistic nature cruelly confined by the circumstances of her life.

Raphael slid into the driver's seat of the car, closing the door and then starting the engine.

The town council had been only too delighted to allow him to finance the restoration work on the garden, and to hand the whole project over to him. Had there been a trace of fear in their response to him as well as delighted gratitude? They knew his family history as well as he did himself. They knew that it involved broken lives and bodies, and the inheritance of blood that belonged to a name that still today caused shudders amongst those who whispered it in secret with fear and loathing. Beccelli! Who, knowing the history of that name, would not shrink from it?

He could not do so, however, Raphael reminded himself as he drove. He was forced every day of his life to face what he was, what he carried within him and its capacity for cruelty and evil. It was an inheritance that tortured and tormented those not strong enough to carry it. Those who, like his mother, had ended up taking their own life out of the despair that knowing they carried such genes had brought. Raphael stiffened against the unwanted emotional intrusion of his own thoughts. He had decided a long time ago that no one would ever be allowed to know how he felt about his blood inheritance or the ghosts of his past. Let others judge him as they wished; he would never allow himself to be vulnerable enough to let them see what he really felt. He would never seek their advice or acknowledge their criticism. He had been left alone to carry the burden of what he was, his father having drowned in a sailing accident and his mother dead by her own hand—both of them gone within a year of one another just as he had entered his teens.

Until he had come of age trustees had managed the complex intricacies of his inheritance and its wealth. A succession of relatives— aunts, uncles, cousins—had made room for him under their roofs whilst he was growing up. After all, he was the head of the family whether they liked it or not. Its wealth and status, like its patronage, belonged to him alone.

In the way of such things, his great-aunt's death and the consequent gathering of the family had given his relatives an opportunity to bring up the subject of his marriage and the subsequent production of the next heir—a favourite subject for all Italian matriarchs with unmarried offspring.

It was no secret to Raphael that his father's cousin wanted him to marry her daughter, nor that the wife of his only male cousin, Carlo, often wondered if one day her husband or her son might stand in Raphael's shoes, should he not have a son.

Raphael, though, had no intention of enlightening either of them with regard to his plans. And they knew better than to press him too much.

The Beccelli family had been notorious for their cruelty and their temper. Raphael's own fear, however, lay not only with what he might have inherited himself but, even more importantly, with the genes that he would pass on, and those who might inherit them. In this modern world it might be possible to screen out those elements that combined to lead to a new life inheriting physical conditions that might damage it, but as yet there was no test that could pinpoint the inheritance of a mental and emotional mindset that would revel in cruelty, or protect a new life from the inner burden that came from knowing one's history.

They were travelling through the gathering darkness of the spring evening, and it was minutes before Charley caught a glimpse of a road sign that sent her heart thudding with renewed anxiety. She realised that they were going in the opposite direction from her expected destination.

This isn't the way to the airport,' she protested

'No.'

'Stop this car immediately. I want to get out.'

'Don't be ridiculous.'

'I am not being ridiculous. You have as good as kidnapped me, and my boss is expecting me to be back in England tomorrow.'

'Not any more,' Raphael informed her. 'When I spoke to him earlier he was most anxious that you should remain here—in fact he begged me to keep you and use you for whatever purpose I wished.'

Charley opened her mouth to object to the offensive connotations of his choice of words, and then closed it again when she saw the gleam in his eyes. He wanted to upset and humiliate her. Well, she wouldn't give him the satisfaction of letting him think that he had done so.

Instead she said firmly, 'You said that you have taken over the project?'

'Yes. I have decided to fund the restoration myself rather than allow my family's name to be connected with the kind of cheap, tawdry restoration you had in mind.'

'So you'll be cancelling our contract, then?'

'I would certainly like to do so,' Raphael agreed. 'But unfortunately it won't be possible for me to do that and find someone else to complete the work in time for next year's formal re-opening of the garden. However, I do have some concerns about your suitability to manage the project.'

She was going to be sacked.

'It seems to me that someone who gave up her Fine Arts degree halfway through to study accountancy instead is not the person to manage this project in the way I wish to have it managed.'

'My career choices have nothing to do with you,' Charley defended herself. She certainly wasn't going to tell him that after the deaths of their parents and the financial problems that had followed she had felt morally obliged to train for something that would enable her to earn enough to help her elder sister provide a home for them all.

'On the contrary, since I am now in effect employing you they have a very great deal to do with me. From now on you will work directly under my control and you will be answerable directly to me. Should I find that you are not able to satisfy me and meet the standards I set, then you will be dismissed. Your employer has already assured me that he has someone in mind to replace you, should that prove necessary.'

'His daughter,' Charley was unable to stop herself from saying furiously, 'who can't speak a word of Italian.'

Ignoring her outburst, Raphael continued, 'It is my intention that the garden will be restored as exactly as possible to its original design.'

Charley stared at him in the darkness of the car, the light from the moon revealing the harsh pride of his profile, etching it with silver instead of charcoal.

'But that will cost a fortune,' she protested, 'and that's just for starters. Finding craftsmen to undertake the work—'

'You can leave that to me. I have connections with a committee in Florence that is responsible for much of the work on its heritage buildings; it owes me favours.'

And she could just bet that calling in 'favours' was something he was very, very good at doing, Charley recognised.

'Your work begins tomorrow, when we will visit the site together. I have in my possession the original plans.'

'Tomorrow? But I was only supposed to be here for the day. I haven't got anywhere to stay, or…'

'That will not be a problem. You will stay at the *palazzo*, so that I can monitor your work and ensure that the garden is restored exactly as I wish. That is where we are going now—unless, of course, it is your wish that I ask your employer to send someone else to take over from you?'

Was that secretly what he was hoping? Well, he was going to be disappointed, Charley decided proudly. She was as equally capable of managing a high-budget project as she was of managing a low-budget one, and in truth there was nothing she would have enjoyed more than seeing the garden come to life as it had once been, if only *he* was not involved. More important than any of that, though, was her need to keep on earning the money they all so desperately needed right now. She could not afford the luxury of pride, no matter how much it irked her.

The road began to climb up ahead of them, and on the hilltop, caught in the full beam of the rising moon, Charley could see the vast bulk of an imposing building dominating the landscape.

'That is the Palazzo Raverno up ahead,' Raphael informed her.

The façade of the building was illuminated by floodlights, and when they had finally came to a halt outside it Charley could see it was Baroque in style, with curved pediments and intricate mouldings displaying the deliberate interplay between curvaceous forms and straight lines that was so much a part of the Baroque style of architecture.

Despite her determination not to betray what she was feeling, when Raphael got out of the car and then came round to the passenger door to open it for her she was totally unable to stop herself from saying in disbelief, as she followed him up the marble steps, 'You live here? In this?'

Her awed gaze took in the magnificence of the building in front of her. It looked like something that should have belonged to the National Trust, or whatever the Italian equivalent of that organisation was.

'Since it is the main residence of the Duke

of Raverno, and has been since it was first re-modelled and designated as such in the seven-teenth century, yes, I do live here—although sometimes I find it more convenient to stay in my apartments in Rome or Florence, depend-ing on what business I am conducting.' He shrugged dismissively, making Charley even more aware of the vast gulf that lay between their ways of life.

'My nephews would envy you having some-where so large to play in,' was all she could manage to say. 'They complain that there isn't enough room in the house we all share for them to play properly with their toys.'

'You *all* share? Does that mean that you live with your sister and her husband?'

Raphael didn't know why he was bothering to ask her such a question, nor why the thought that she might share her day-to-day life with a man, even if he was her own sister's husband, should fill him with such immediate and illogi-cal hostility. What did it matter to him who she lived with?

'Ruby isn't married. The three of us—my eldest sister Lizzie, Ruby and I and the twins—all live together. It was Lizzie's idea. She wanted to keep the family together after our parents died, so she gave up her career in London to come back to Cheshire.'

'And what did you give up?'

The question had Charley looking at him in shock. She hadn't expected it, and had no defences against it.

'Nothing,' she lied, and quickly changed the subject to ask uncertainly, 'Will your wife not mind you bringing me here into her home like this?'

'My wife?'

Raphael had been moving up the marble steps ahead of her, but now he stopped and turned to look at her.

'I do not have a wife,' he informed her, 'and nor do I ever intend to have one.'

Charley was too surprised to stop herself from saying, 'But you're a duke—you must want to have a son, an heir… I mean that's what being someone like a duke is all about, isn't it?'

Something—not merely anger, nor even pride, but something that went beyond both of those things and was darker and scarred with bitterness—was fleetingly visible in his expression before he controlled it. She had seen it, though, and it aroused Charley's curiosity, making her wonder what had been responsible for it.

'You think my whole purpose, the whole focus of my life, my very existence, is to ensure the continuation of my genes?' The grey eyes were burning as hot as molten mercury now. 'Well, I dare say there are plenty of others who share your view, but I certainly do not. I have no intention of marrying—ever—and even less of producing a son or any child, for that matter.'

Charley was too astonished to say anything. It seemed so out of character for the kind of man she had assumed he must be that he should not consider marriage and the production of an heir as the prime reason for his own being. That, surely, was how the aristocracy thought? It was the mindset that had made them what they were—the need, the determination to continue their male line in order to secure and continue their right to enjoy the status and the wealth that had been built up by previous generations. To hear one of their number state otherwise so unequivocally seemed so strange that it immediately made Charley wonder *why* Raphael felt the way he did. Not, of course, that she was ever likely to get the opportunity to ask him. That would require a degree of intimacy and trust between them that could never exist. He was obviously very angry with her—again—and as he took a step towards her Charley took one step back, forgetting that she was standing on a step and immediately losing her balance.

Raphael's reaction was swift, his hands gripping hold of her upper arms punishingly. Not to protect her from any hurt or harm, Charley recognised, but to protect himself from coming into unwanted contact with her.

That knowledge burned her pride and her heart, reminding her of all those other times when men had dismissed her as being unworthy of their interest.

'You should take more care, Charlotte Wareham.'

'It's not Charlotte, it's Charley,' she corrected him, tilting her chin defiantly as she did so.

He was still holding her, and once again out of nowhere she was having to fight against the shock of suddenly experiencing an awareness of him that was totally alien to her nature. How could it have happened? she wondered dizzily. She just didn't feel like this ever—going hot and then cold, trembling with awareness, burning with the heat of sensation surging through her body as it reacted to his maleness.

She had taught herself years ago not to be interested in men, because she had always known that they were not interested in her.

She wasn't sure when she had first realised that in her parents' eyes she wasn't as pretty as either of her siblings. Once she had realised it, though, she had quickly learned to play up to the role of tomboy that they had given her, pretending not to mind when her mother bought pretty dresses for her sisters and jeans for her, pretending that being the family tomboy was what she actually wanted, telling herself that it would be silly for her to try to mimic her sisters when she was so much plainer than they were. It had been her father who had first started calling her 'Charley'—a name that suited a tomboy far better than Charlotte.

Over the years she had learned that the best way to protect herself from comments about her own lack of femininity and prettiness when compared with her sisters was to ensure that others believed she *wanted* to be what she was—that she wanted to be Charley and not Charlotte. But now, for some unknown reason, with Raphael's fingers curling into her flesh, his ice-cold grey gaze boring into her as though his scrutiny was penetrating her most private thoughts and fears, she felt a sharp stab of pain for what she was—and what she was not. If she had been either her elder sister Lizzie, with her elegance and her classically beautiful features, or her younger sister Ruby, with her mop of thick tousled curls and the piquant beauty of her face, he would not be looking at her as he was—as though he wanted to push her away from him and reject her.

Being so close to him was unnerving her—the sheer solid steel strength of his male body brutally hard against her own unprepared softness. Unwittingly her gaze absorbed the olive warmth of his throat above the collar of his shirt and then lifted upwards, sucked into a vortex of instinct beyond her control, blinding her senses to everything else as she fastened on the angle of his jaw, the pores in his skin, the shadow where a beard would grow if he wasn't clean-shaven. She wanted to lift her hand and touch him there on his face, to see if she could feel some slight roughness or if his skin was as smooth and polished as it looked. Her gaze lingered and darted across his face with lightning speed, swift as a child let loose in a sweet shop, eager to gather up forbidden pleasures as fast as it could.

How she longed to be set free to draw and paint this man's image on canvas, to capture the essence of his pride and arrogance so that all that he was, inside and out, was revealed, leaving him as vulnerable as neatly as he had just stripped her of her own defences. That mouth alone said so much about him. It was hard and cruel, the top lip sharply cut. In her mind's eye Charley was already visualising her own sketch of it, so engrossed in what was going on inside her head that when she looked at his bottom lip to assess its shape it was the artist within her that did that assessing, and not the woman. It was the woman, though, whose breath was dragged into her lungs and whose awareness was not of the lines and structure of flesh and muscle, but instead of the openly sensual curve and fullness of his lips. What must it be like to be kissed by a man with such a mouth? Would he kiss with the cruelty of that harshly cut top lip, demanding and taking his own pleasure? Or would he kiss with the sensual promise of that bottom lip, taking the woman he was kissing to a place where pleasure was a foregone conclusion and all she would need to measure it was the depth to which she allowed that pleasure to take her?

Charley's throat locked round the betraying sound of her awareness of him that rose in her throat, stifling and suppressing it. She pulled back stiffly within his hold, causing Raphael to immediately want to keep her where she was. Why? Because for a fraction of a second his body had reacted to her with physical desire? That meant nothing. It had been a momentary automatic reaction—that was all; nothing more. Raphael purposely kept his dealings with women confined to relationships in which both people understood certain rules about their intimacy being purely sexual and nothing more. He was committed to remaining single and child-free as a matter of duty and honour, and nothing was ever going to change that. Certainly not this woman.

And yet beneath his grip Raphael could feel the slenderness of her arm, and just registering that was enough to cause his thoughts to turn to how soft her skin would be, how pale and tender, with delicate blue veins running up from her wrist, the pulse of her blood quickening in them as he touched her. Her naked body would look as though it were carved from alabaster: milk-white and silkily warm to the touch.

Furious with himself for the direction his thoughts had taken, Raphael pushed the tempting vision away, ignoring the eager hunger that was beginning to pulse through his body.

It was irrational and impossible that he should desire her. Even her name affronted his aesthetic senses and his love of beauty.

'Charley. That is a boy's name and you are a woman,' he pointed out to her, and then demanded, 'Why do you reject your womanhood?'

'I don't—I'm not,' Charley protested defensively. Why hadn't he let go of her? She knew that he wanted to do so. She could see it in his eyes, in the curl of his mouth, so cold and potentially cruel, and yet... A shudder of sensation she couldn't control swept through her as she looked at his mouth. What would it be like to be kissed by a man like him? To be held, and touched, caressed, wanted...?

A small sound locked her throat, her eyes darkening to such a dense blue-green that the colour reminded Raphael of the deep, clean, untouched waters in the small private bay below the villa he owned on the island of Sicily. The sudden swift hardening of his body before he had time to check its reaction to her caught him off guard, making him deride himself mentally for his reaction. He couldn't *possibly* desire her, he told himself grimly. It was unthinkable.

'No Italian woman would dress herself as you do, nor hold herself as you do, without any pride in her womanhood.'

He was being deliberately cruel to her,

Charley decided. He must be able to see, after all, that she did not have the kind of womanhood it was possible to take pride in. She was plain and lanky, unfeminine and undesirable— so much the complete opposite to the beauty her artistic senses admired and longed to create that it hurt her to know how far short she fell of her own standards. Secretly, growing up, she had believed that if she could not be beautiful then she could at least create beauty. But even that had been denied her. It was a sacrifice she had made willingly, for the sake of her sisters. They loved her as she was, and she loved them. That was what mattered—not this man.

And yet when he released her and was no longer touching her, when he looked at her as though he despised her, it *did* matter, Charley recognised miserably.

Following Raphael into the *palazzo*, Charley was conscious of how untidy and unattractive she must look, in cheap jeans that had never fitted properly, even when she had first bought them, and the bulky, out-of-shape navy jumper she had thought she might need if she had to visit the site, which she had worn over her tee shirt to allow her more packing space in her backpack. And her shoes were so worn that no amount of polishing could make them look anything other than shabby. But then she forgot her awful clothes as she took in the magnificence of the large entrance hall, with its frescoed wall panels and ceiling, the colours surely as rich and fresh today as they had been when they had first been painted, making her want to reach out and touch them, to feel that richness beneath her fingertips. The scenes were allegorical—relating, she guessed, to Roman mythology rather than Christianity—and had obviously been painted by a master hand. Just looking at them was a feast for her senses, overwhelming them and bringing emotional tears to her eyes that she was quick to blink away, not wanting Raphael to see them. She tried to focus on something else, but even the marble staircase that rose up from the hallway was a work of art in its own right.

Raphael, who had been watching her, saw

her eyes widen and change colour, her face lifting towards the frescoes with an awed joy that illuminated her features and revealed the true beauty of the delicate bone structure.

His heart slammed into his ribs with a force for which he was totally unprepared. The fresco was one of his personal favourites, and her silent but open homage to it echoed his own private feelings. But how could it be possible that this woman of all people, whose behaviour said that she had no awareness of or respect for artistic beauty, should look at the fresco and react to it with all that he felt for it himself? It shouldn't have been possible. It should not have happened. But it had, and he had witnessed it. Raphael watched her lift her hand as she took a step towards the nearest fresco, as though unable to stop herself, and then let it fall back. He hadn't expected it of her. She hadn't struck him as someone who was capable of feeling, never mind expressing such an emotion, and yet now he could feel her passion filling the distance between them.

If he looked at her now he knew he would see her eyes had darkened to that stormy blue-green that had caught his attention earlier, and her lips would be pressed together—soft, sensual pillows of flesh, too full to form a flat line, tempting any man who looked at them to taste them…

Raphael cursed himself under his breath. He had been without a lover for too long. But he couldn't remember ever seeing anyone react quite so emotionally to the frescoes other than his mother, who had loved them and passed on that love to him. He could still remember how as a small child she had lifted him and held him so that he could see the frescos at close quarters, her voice filled with emotion as she talked to him about them. His life had been so happy then, so filled with love and security—before he had known about his dark inheritance.

So much beauty, Charley thought achingly. Her heart, indeed the very essence of her had gone hungry for such beauty for so long. In her imagination she tried to comprehend what it must have been like to be the pupil of such an artist, to have the privilege of watching him at work, knowing that one's own best efforts could never hope to match his smallest brushstrokes, feeding off the joy of witnessing such artistry. Only of course the great masters had never taken on female pupils—not even tomboy female pupils.

Once she had dreamed of working amongst great works of art in one of London's famous museums, as an art historian, but that dream had come to an end with her parents' death.

Dragging her gaze from the frescoes, she shook her head like someone coming out of a deep dream and said slowly to Raphael, 'Giovanni Battista Zelotti, the most famous of all fresco painters of his era. He would never tell anyone the recipe he used for his famous blue paint, and the secret died with him.'

Raphael nodded his head. 'My ancestor commissioned him after he had seen the fresco he painted for the Medicis in Florence.'

He looked at his watch, his movement

catching Charley's attention. His wrists were muscular, and the dark hairs on his arm underlined his maleness, making her stomach muscles tighten into a slow ache that permeated the whole of her lower body. What would it be like to be touched, held by such a man? To know the polished, controlled expertise of his stroke against her skin…? And he would be an expert at knowing what gave a woman the most pleasure… The slow ache flared into something more intense, causing Charley to catch her breath as she tried to hold her own against her body's attack on her defences. It must be Italy that was making her feel like this—Italy, and the knowledge that she was so close to the cities she had longed to visit and their wonderful art treasures, not Raphael himself. That could not be—must not be.

CHAPTER THREE

WARMTH, sunshine, a scent on the air coming in through the open balcony windows that was both unfamiliar and enticing, and a large bed with the most wonderful sheets she had ever slept in. And despite everything she had slept, Charley admitted as she luxuriated guiltily in the delicious comfort of the bed and her surroundings, having been woken only minutes earlier by a discreet knock on her bedroom door, followed by the entrance of a smiling young maid with Charley's breakfast.

When Raphael's housekeeper had brought her up here last night she had felt slightly daunted, but to her relief Anna, as she had told Charley she must call her, had quickly put her at her ease, organising a light meal for her, and telling her that breakfast would be sent up to her room for her because 'Il Duce—' as she had referred to Raphael '—takes his breakfast very early when he is here, so that he can go out and speak to the men whilst they are working with the vines.'

Charley was, of course, relieved that she didn't have to have breakfast with Raphael, and it wasn't because she was curious about him in any way at all that as she left the bed she was drawn to the balcony windows and the view of the vines she had already seen beyond the gardens that lay immediately below them. Slipping the band she used to tie her hair back off her face over her wrist, Charley padded barefoot to the balcony in her strappy sleep top with matching shorts—a Christmas present from the twins. The outfit was loose on her, due to the weight she had lost over these last anxious weeks.

It was wonderful to feel the warmth of the sun on her bare skin. Charley turned her face up towards it, and then tensed as she heard

Raphael's voice and then saw him appear round the corner of the building, accompanied by another man with whom he was deep in conversation. Both men were dressed casually, in short-sleeved shirts and chinos, but it was to Raphael that her attention was drawn as the two men shook hands and the older man began to walk away, leaving Raphael standing alone. The blue linen of his shirt emphasised the tanned flesh of his bare forearms. A beam of sunlight touched the strong column of his throat. Charley had to curl her fingers in an attempt to quell the longing itching in them— not a desire to pick up a piece of charcoal and sketch his lean, erotically male lines, but instead a desire to touch him, to feel the warmth of the life force that lay beneath his flesh, to experience how it felt to be free to physically explore such a man.

Beneath the thin cotton jersey of her top her nipples tightened, the small movement she made instinctively in rejection of her arousal dragging the fabric against their swollen sensitivity, conjuring up inside her head images of a male touch creating—indeed inciting— that sensitivity and then harvesting its sensuality, teasing her with skilled, tormenting caresses that played on her arousal, drawing it from her, making her want a closer intimacy. Behind her closed eyelids Charley could almost see the dark male hands tormenting her, making her yearn for their possession of her breasts. Instinctively she stepped forward—and then gasped, her eyes opening as she came up against the balcony railing.

Down below her Raphael looked up towards the balcony. It was too late for her to step back out of sight. He had seen her, and he would know that she had seen him. Suddenly conscious of how she must look, dressed in her sleepwear and with her hair all over the place, she plucked at the hairband on her wrist, her eyes widening in dismay as it slipped from her fingers and dropped through the railings, landing almost at Raphael's feet.

When he bent to pick it up Charley could see the fabric of his linen shirt stretch across his shoulders. It was such a male thing that—the breadth of a man's shoulders, the way his body tapered down in a muscular V-shape towards his hips, his chest hard and packed with muscles where her own was soft with the rounded shape of her breasts.

Raphael was straightening up, putting her hairband in his pocket, looking up at her, at her hair, her mouth, her breasts. Charley's toes curled into the mosaic-tiled floor of the balcony as she sucked in her stomach against the heat that flooded over her.

A mobile phone began to ring. Raphael's, she recognised as he removed it from his pocket and began to speak into it, turning his back to her and then beginning to walk away.

It was the warmth of the sun on her sunshine-starved body that had aroused her, not Raphael. He had just happened to be there at the same time—that was all, Charley insisted to herself as she stood under the shower, de-

terminedly not thinking of anything other than
the reason she was here in Italy.

Ten minutes later, having searched through
her backpack three times, Charley dropped it
onto the floor in defeat. How could she not
have put in a couple of spare hairbands? She
never wore her hair loose. *Never.* She preferred, *needed* to have it tied back and under
control. She simply wasn't feminine enough to
wear her hair loose in a mass of curls.

His call over, Raphael looked down at the
hairband he had removed from his pocket, his
body hardening as he studied it. Inside his
head he could see Charlotte Wareham standing
on the balcony, the bright morning sunshine
turning the top and shorts she was wearing
virtually transparent so that he could see quite
plainly the flesh beneath them—her breasts
round and full, shadowed by the dark aureole
of flesh from which her nipples rose to push
against the fabric covering them. How differ-

ent she had appeared then, without the concealment of the shapeless clothes she had been wearing the previous day. Raphael tried to dismiss the erotic image from inside his head, but instead his memory produced another picture, this time of Charlotte Wareham pressed against the balcony, her back arched, her eyes closed in a mixture of surrender and enticement, those long, long legs of hers parted, the sunlight revealing the neat covering of hair that protected her sex. How easy it would have been for a man to slide his hand up her thigh and beneath the cuff of her shorts, so that he could stroke that sensual softness and explore what it concealed. What she had been wearing—two small plain items of clothing, not suggestive at all, so one might think—had cloaked her body in such a way that their mere presence and proximity to her body had filled him with a fierce urgency to feast on all the delights her flesh had seemed to offer. He couldn't accuse her of being deliberately provocative, Raphael knew, and it brought a sharp edge to his irritation with himself to have to admit that against all the odds, and certainly against his normal code of behaviour, his mind had somehow developed a will of its own and had transformed clothes so ordinary into garments filled with sensual promise. Just remembering now the way in which the thin shoulder straps of her top had suggested they could be easily slid down her arms, to reveal the full promise of those dark hard nipples, filled him with angry rejection of his body's response to her. The soft, unstructured shape of the top itself, which had finished almost on her waist, revealing a glimmer of pale flesh, had urged him to lift it up and push it out of the way, so that he could see and touch the promised soft lushness of her body. And the shorts, baggy and loose-legged… A man could take his pleasure exploring whatever part of her he chose to reveal, knowing that he had the whole of her to access as and when and how he chose to do so.

Cursing himself silently again, Raphael

commanded his self-control to dispel both his thoughts and the arousal they were creating. If he needed a woman then there were plenty available to him who would make more suitable bedmates than Charlotte Wareham.

Charley longed to fasten her hair and hold it gripped off her face as she stood in front of the desk behind which Raphael was seated. She had been summoned to his presence like a miscreant about to be punished—which, of course, as far as he was concerned was exactly what she was. She couldn't touch her hair, no matter how uncomfortable she felt with it tumbling down onto her shoulders, because if she did it might remind Raphael, and would certainly remind her, of the circumstances in which she had lost her hairband.

In an attempt to distract herself she studied her surroundings. The fact that the large room was on the ground floor of the *palazzo* indicated that its original purpose would have been for business to be conducted: orders given, favours sought and deals made—the administrative centre of the ducal estate.

The ceiling was decorated with painted lozenges depicting various hereditary arms and symbols. The polished wood of the library shelving which held huge leather-covered books, their gold lettering gleaming softly, added to the imposing air of the room. Traditionally it would no doubt have been here where those who administered the estate would come to present their accounts to the duke, to answer his questions and receive his praise—or his wrath.

Charley shivered. There was no doubt which of those things Raphael believed she deserved.

The heavy, ornately carved and inlaid desk, positioned to make the most of the light coming in through the narrow windows, was covered in papers.

Raphael looked briefly at Charley. She was wearing her hair down, and the sight of it, freshly washed, the delicately scented smell of it and of her reawakened the desire he had felt earlier. What was the matter with him? He was no mere hormone-driven boy, to be tempted and tormented by the thought of sliding his hands into those thick wild curls, of lacing his fingers through them as he covered her naked body with his own, arousing her as she had aroused him. Using the determination with which he had always so ruthlessly crushed any challenge or resistance to his self-control, Raphael closed down his unwanted thoughts as firmly as though he had trapped them behind an impregnable steel door. To allow himself to feel desire for Charlotte Wareham would be unacceptably inappropriate behaviour and, more than that, a weakness within himself that he was not prepared to tolerate. He had no idea why she should have such an effect on him. She was neither groomed nor elegant. She was not witty or sophisticated. In short, there was nothing about her that should have had any appeal for him.

All he could think was that somehow his body had been confused by the anger she

aroused within him and was thus acting inap-
propriately. The reality was that Charlotte
Wareham was proving to be a thorn in his side
in more ways than one.

'I have copies here of the original plans for
the garden. I want you to study them and see
what is to be done within the garden.'

'Yes, Il Duce.' Charley responded through
gritted teeth.

There was a small, dangerous silence, as
though he knew how she had almost choked
on delivering the title that in her own estimation reduced her to little more than a slave,
forced to do his bidding, and how she had
spoken the words with her angry contempt.
She could see the thunder in the now dark grey
eyes and she waited, knowing that she would
be punished.

But when he spoke he shocked her by saying
dismissively, 'You will address me as Raphael
and not Il Duce.'

Use his name and not his title? Charley
almost told him that she would do no such

thing, but just in time realised how ridiculous such a piece of defiance would be.

'Now,' he continued, 'let me assure you that any attempt on your part to despoil the restoration of the garden with items of the sort I saw yesterday will result in your immediate dismissal. The garden will be restored to its full glory in every detail.'

Charley could almost feel the intensity of his commitment. If he could make that kind of commitment to a garden then how much more intense would be the commitment he made to the woman he loved?

Her body convulsed on a small betraying shiver. Once, a long, long time ago as a girl, before she had realised that tomboys were not the kind of girls the male sex wanted to protect, she had dreamed of growing up and being loved by a man whose love for her would be so strong that it would protect her always.

An aching sense of painful loss filled her. She would never know that kind of love— Raphael's kind of love.

Love? What on earth was going on? Love and this man had no place together in her thoughts. No place at all. She could not afford to be vulnerable. She was too vulnerable already.

A discreet but firm rap on the door broke across her thoughts and had Raphael turning towards it, commanding, 'Come.' It opened to admit his serious-looking male PA, Ciro, whom Charley had met earlier, when he had introduced himself to her and told her that Raphael was waiting to speak with her.

Ciro spoke quickly and quietly to Raphael, causing him to frown slightly and then tell her, 'I have to go and speak with the manager of the vineyard. I shall not be long. Ciro will arrange for Anna to have some coffee sent in for you whilst you wait for me to return.'

His words sounded polite enough, but Charley wasn't deceived. What they really were was an order to her that she was to remain here until his return—when no doubt she would be subjected to more contempt and more verbal castigation, she decided as Raphael strode through the door his PA was holding open for him, leaving Ciro to follow him.

Thanking the maid for the coffee she had just brought, Charley picked up the cup the girl had filled for her, wrapping both her hands around it for comfort—like a child holding a comfort rag or toy, Charley thought, deriding herself for her own vulnerability.

As a child it had always seemed that she had been the one to get the blame for the accidentally naughty things the three of them had sometimes done—even when Lizzie had insisted that the fault was hers. There had been many times when she had gone to bed at night crying into her pillow in silent misery, feeling misunderstood, feeling she was less worthy of parental love than her two sisters. Now the way Raphael was treating her had evoked some of that long-ago misery and sense of injustice, adding to her existing despair.

She took a quick gulp of her coffee and then

got up from her chair, putting the cup down as she was drawn to the sketches and plans laid out on Raphael's desk. Since they were of the pleasure garden, there was no reason why she should not look at them, she assured herself. She had, after all, seen the plans before, at home in England.

These, though, were not modern drawings, but sketches and watercolours of parts of the original garden, Charley quickly recognised, immediately becoming so absorbed in them that everything else was forgotten as she was mentally swept back to another century, enviously imagining what it must have been like to be involved in such a wonderful project. The plans and sketches alone were minor works of art in their own right, and Charley's fingertips trembled as she touched the papers on which those long-ago craftsmen had etched their sketches and detailed measurements of fountains, statues, colonnades and grottos.

A perspective overview showed the full layout of the garden. The formal sweep of a curved, colonnaded entrance opened in the centre, to draw the eye down a wide avenue planted with what looked like pleached limes. Either side of it the garden was intersected by narrower walkways, opening out into sheltered bowers decorated with seats and statuary, beyond which lay a stone fountain, in the middle of which was a huge piece of statuary. A paved terrace shaded by vines marked the boundary, where the land fell away with a view over an ornamental lake, complete with a grotto.

There were sketches for small, elegant pavilions, 'secret' water gardens designed to spring into life when the unsuspecting walked close to them. Charley ached with longing to have seen the garden following its completion. Raphael was right to say that trying to recreate such beauty using cheap manmade materials was an insult to the original artists.

She was so wrapped up in the world those long-ago craftsmen and artists had created that she didn't hear the soft click of the door opening, and was oblivious to Raphael's return and the fact that he was standing watching her as she stood looking down at the papers on his desk, her expression one of absorbed intensity.

Charley lifted her gaze from the desk, her eyes shadowed with all that she was feeling, lost in her own world—only to come abruptly out of that world when she saw Raphael.

How long had he been there? The way he was looking at her made her feel acutely vulnerable. She stepped back from the desk, so intent on escaping from his gaze that she forgot about the small table behind her on which the maid had placed the tray of coffee.

As she bumped into the table she dislodged the heavy thermos jug. Before she had time to react Raphael had reacted for her, reaching her side, pulling her away from the table just as hot coffee spouted from the jug and onto her jean-clad thigh.

She must have cried out, although she wasn't aware of having done so, because immediately Raphael looked down to where the hot liquid had soaked through her jeans, his sharp and almost accusatory, 'You have been burned,' causing Charley to shake her head.

'No. I'm all right,' she insisted.

Her face was burning with a mixture of emotions. Her leg was stinging painfully beneath the wet fabric of her jeans, but it was her own embarrassment at having been so clumsy rather than any pain that was making her feel so self-conscious. There was a small puddle of coffee on the snow-white starched linen tray cloth with its discreet monogram, and coffee on the floor as well, but thankfully it had missed the rug that covered part of the marble-tiled floor. Her parents would have shaken their heads if they had witnessed her mishap, pointing out to her that she was dreadfully clumsy. How she had longed to be deft and delicate in her movements, and not like the baby elephant her mother had always teasingly told her she was.

'It's my own fault,' she told Raphael. 'I shouldn't be so clumsy.'

Clumsy? Raphael frowned. She was tall, yes,

but her hands and her feet were elegantly narrow, her body far too slender for her ever to be 'clumsy'. In fact if anything Raphael had noticed how controlled and economical her movements were, almost as though she was afraid to express herself.

'You'll want to get changed. I'll wait for you down here.'

'There's no need for me to change,' Charley told him. 'My jeans will dry.'

He was looking at her in a way that said very explicitly what he thought of a woman who cared so little for her appearance that she was content to continue wearing jeans that were stained with and smelled of coffee.

Gritting her teeth, Charley lowered her pride to admit, 'I haven't got anything to change into, since you insisted that I was to stay here instead of going home and then returning.'

Now that the immediate shock was receding Charley was beginning to realise that the scalding coffee had hurt her more than she had first thought. Her leg was throbbing and burning, the pain growing more intense with every passing second, but she was stubbornly determined not to let Raphael see that.

'Go up to your room,' Raphael commanded. 'I'll speak to Anna about providing you with something to wear for now.'

It was easier to give in than to argue—especially with the pain growing more intense by the second, Charley admitted as she stood up. And then, to her shock, she felt her burned leg give way beneath her, causing her to stumble into Raphael's desk.

Raphael was on his feet immediately, opening a drawer in his desk, coming towards her as she clung to the edge of the desktop for support.

'No!' Charley protested, and protested a second time as she saw the scissors in his hand. But it was no use. He was cutting through the wet denim as ruthlessly as he would have cut down an enemy. The cool air on her burned flesh caused Charley to shudder. She felt slightly sick and light-headed when she looked at her leg and saw how the flesh had reddened and blistered.

Raphael's mouth tightened as he looked at the burned flesh. 'This needs proper medical treatment,' he announced grimly.

'No. I'm all right,' Charley insisted. 'I'll go upstairs and bathe it with some cool water.' She let go of the desk and took a couple of steps, the blood draining from her face as her body responded with a surge of pain.

Raphael had seen enough. Of all the stubborn, stupid women… Before Charley could stop him he was lifting her into his arms, his action forcing her to hold on to him tightly by putting her arms around his neck. He couldn't possibly be intending to carry her all the way to her room—but it seemed that he was, and Charley could only guess at the power in the muscles cloaked by his fine linen shirt as he did so, as effortlessly as though she weighed little more than a child.

Once they were inside her room, Raphael placed her on the bed and then, after instructing her not to move, he left.

Strange how the pain had subsided whilst she was in Raphael's arms. But it had returned now, and if anything was even worse. It was ridiculous for her to feel as though she had been abandoned, and even more ridiculous— dangerously so—for her to wish that Raphael had stayed with her. Charley looked down at her lower body which, unlike her damaged leg, was still encased in her jeans. She wasn't helpless, she reminded herself. She sat up and started to ease her jeans off, wincing as the fabric brushed against her burned flesh.

'What the devil…? I told you not to move.'

Charley swung round. Raphael was coming towards her, carrying a first aid box.

'I've rung the doctor, and he should be here soon, but in the meantime the burn needs to be covered by a dressing.'

Raphael was kneeling on the floor next to her now bare legs, apparently oblivious to the fact that she had removed her jeans and was now only covered by the lacy briefs which had been Lizzie's Christmas present to her.

'There's really no need...' she began, but Raphael stopped her.

'On the contrary—there is every need,' he told her.

She had removed her jeans, and now it wasn't just the slender length of her legs that was distracting him from his self-imposed task, Raphael acknowledged. He had seen women wearing far more provocative and re-vealing underwear than the lacy briefs that Charley was wearing, but right now the fact that he was acutely aware of what lay beneath the barrier concealing her body from him was having a very unwanted effect on him physi-cally. Angry with himself for allowing his body to overcome his self-control, Raphael worked quickly to open the medical kit and remove the necessary dressing, keeping his gaze fixed firmly on the burned flesh of Charley's thigh, which had now begun to tremble slightly.

'The pain is getting worse?' he demanded.

Charley nodded her head. It was, after all,

true that the pain was bad, but it was also true that it wasn't the pain that was causing her body to tremble. Nor was it the reason that the trembling increased when Raphael placed the dressing on her bare flesh. Her reaction to his touch horrified her. She was behaving like an adolescent with a crush.

'There—that should protect the burn until the doctor gets here to look at it properly.'

Charley nodded her head, managing a reluctant, 'Thank you.'

She felt shivery and sick, her nerves jangling—and not, she suspected, purely because of her burned thigh. This time it was a relief when Raphael left her.

CHAPTER FOUR

IT WAS another lovely sunny morning, her second here in Italy, in Raphael's *palazzo*, in what was in effect his bedroom, since he owned the *palazzo*. Goosebumps rose on her skin as though it had been touched, caressed. Helplessly Charley closed her eyes. It must be the painkillers the doctor had given her yesterday, after he had looked at her burn, re-dressed it and pronounced that she must spend the rest of the day in bed, not her wayward thoughts of Raphael.

She knew better this morning than to go and stand on the balcony in her sleepwear.

Instead of worrying about who owned the bed she slept in, what she should be doing was worrying about how she was going to manage without her jeans—the one and only garment she had with her to clothe the lower half of her body. She could hardly appear in public in the loose pyjama shorts she was currently wearing, although Raphael had said that he would speak to Anna on her behalf.

She owed Raphael a debt of gratitude for dealing with the situation so properly and promptly. The doctor had told her that the burn could have turned very nasty indeed if it had been left unattended, as she would have chosen to do left to her own devices. Luckily it was not so severe that she would need skin grafts, but he had warned her that she might end up with an area of flesh that would forever be vulnerable to heat and sunlight.

Charley looked at her untouched breakfast tray. She was too on edge to eat. She pushed her hand into her hair to lift it off her face. She had lost a great deal since coming to Italy: her hairband, her jeans, her pride and even some of her self-respect. And hadn't she forgotten something? her conscience prodded. Charley defended her omission. Wasn't the list she had just given herself long enough? Did she really have to add to it that she was also in danger of losing the protection she had put in place around and within herself to stop her from feeling the pain of not being good enough, not being woman enough to merit male attention?

She looked round the room, desperate to find something she could focus on that would enable her to avoid dealing with what was happening to her. The room must have been re-modelled at some stage, because its Baroque decor belonged to a later age than the *palazzo* itself. The softly painted grey-blue wooden panelling was decorated with gilded swags and cupids, and heraldic arms were carved into the imposing bedhead. Her bathroom contained a huge claw-footed bath, in addition to a more modern shower, and the room's walls were tiled in marble.

She heard someone knock on the bedroom door and, assuming it was the maid coming to collect her untouched breakfast tray, went to open the door for her—only to discover that the person standing outside the door was not a maid, but Raphael. As he stepped into the room and closed the door behind him Charley saw that he was carrying a large, not very deep square box, stamped with an international delivery service's label, beneath his arm.

'Are you still in pain?' he asked. 'Dr Scarlarti has left with me some more medication if that is the case.'

Charley wasn't a fan of taking any kind of medication unless it was strictly necessary, so she shook her head, answering him truthfully, 'The skin is still slightly sore, but no more than that.'

The fact that he was in her room fully dressed, whilst she was wearing little more than a vest top and a pair of shorts not intended for public view, was making her feel far more uncomfortable than the burn on her leg. Raphael, on the other hand, looked perfectly at ease—but then Charley suspected he was far more used to being in a bedroom with a member of the opposite sex than she was. Just looking at him was enough to tell her that he was a sexually experienced man who must have shared his life and his bed with any number of willing women.

She gave an involuntary glance towards the bed, where Raphael had deposited the box he had been carrying, unable to stop her imagination from providing her with an image of him on a wide double bed, with the woman he had just pleasured lying in his arms. Her body had started to ache with heavy, sensual longing, and a pulse was beginning to beat low down in her body. A fierce stab of envy whipped through her. Somehow she managed to drag her gaze away from the bed, but looking at Raphael wasn't doing anything to banish either her inappropriate thoughts or the desire they were causing—far from it. How could she be experiencing something like this? It was humiliating—and dangerous.

It took Raphael's crisp, 'Why haven't you eaten your breakfast?' to bring her back to reality, turning her aching desire into prickly defensiveness.

'I wasn't hungry,' she told him.

'We've got a busy day ahead of us, and several acres of abandoned pleasure garden to walk through, provided your leg isn't causing you any pain, and that's something you won't be able to do on an empty stomach. I'll tell Anna to send up a fresh breakfast for you, and then you can meet me downstairs in say an hour's time.'

'I'll have to ask Anna if she can find me something to wear first,' she pointed out.

'That won't be necessary.'

'I can't go out like this,' Charley protested, and then wished she had not as her words caused him to give a probing, prolonged look at her legs. It made her quake inwardly in recognition of how much and how foolishly one part of her wondered what it would be like to have that probing look transformed to one of slow, sensual exploration, followed by the even more sensual stroke of his touch against her skin. Such dangerous, reckless thoughts were not to be encouraged.

'No,' he agreed, coming towards her, causing her to move back and then stop when she realised that she couldn't back up any further because the backs of her legs were already pressed against the bed.

When Raphael stood in front of her and leaned towards her Charley sank down onto the bed, her heart thudding with a mixture of expectation and apprehension, her gaze fixed on the second button of his shirt, not daring to move either up to the tanned bare flesh above it or down to the waistband of his jeans below it. He was reaching towards her—no, not towards her but past her, Charley recognised, dragging her gaze from his chest to his arm just in time to see him retrieving the package he had dropped on the bed earlier.

Mortified by her own misinterpretation of the situation, Charley scrambled to her feet.

'I took the precaution of ordering these for

you,' Raphael was telling her impersonally, handing her the box. 'Hopefully they will fit.'

He was obviously waiting for her to open the parcel—so, turning her back to him as she placed the box back down on the bed, Charley proceeded to do so.

The first thing she noticed once she had removed the carrier's cardboard wrapping was that the elegant black box inside it was stamped in gold with the name of a world-renowned fashion designer. Her heart sank. How on earth was she going to pay for designer jeans?

Uncertainly she opened the box, her anxiety deepening when she realised that the tissue layers inside it didn't just contain a pair of jeans. There was also a tee shirt and what looked like a butter-soft, fashionably shaped tan leather jacket.

Dropping the lid back on the box, Charley turned to confront Raphael.

'I can't possibly wear these clothes,' she told him flatly. 'It's…it's kind of you to have thought of replacing my jeans, but these things…' She gestured helplessly towards the box, embarrassment burning her face. 'They're way outside my price range,' she was forced to tell him. 'I couldn't afford—'

'There is no question of you having to pay for them,' Raphael interrupted.

'What?' Charley was too overwrought to conceal her feelings. 'I can't let you buy clothes for me. It wouldn't be right.'

Raphael crossed his arms and gave her a haughty look of arrogant disdain.

'Where my affairs are concerned, I am the one who says what is and what is not right. I do not intend to waste time in resolving the issue of your tender pride whilst you wait for a member of my staff to source a pair of jeans for you. You will wear the clothes which I have provided. If wearing them is so offensive to you that you do not wish to keep them, when you return to England you may send them back to me—or give them to a charity.'

Charley tried to withstand the look he was

giving her, but it was her gaze that fell away first, even though she managed to muster the determination to tell him, 'The jeans look smaller than my normal size. I don't think they will fit me.'

'On the contrary—they will be a perfect fit,' Raphael told her.

He was so arrogant, so sure of himself, so sure that he was right that Charley had what she knew was a childish urge to puncture that self-confidence.

'You can't possibly know that—even if you checked the size of my own jeans.' Designers were, after all, notorious for making their clothes smaller than those of less expensive manufacturers.

To her shock, instead of backing down Raphael gave her an even more haughty look and told her, 'I didn't need to check your jeans to assess what size you would need. I am a man, and despite the fact that you choose to inflict on your body clothes that smother it instead of enhancing it I am perfectly able to assess the shape and proportions of what lies beneath them.'

What was he saying? That he could see through her clothes to the body she had always been so anxious to protect from male appraisal and criticism? Flustered and defensive, Charley argued fiercely, 'That's not possible.'

Before she could stop him Raphael had taken hold of her—one hand holding her arm and preventing her escape, the other resting on her waist. Charley sucked in her breath. Why hadn't she thought to wear the towelling robe hanging up in her bathroom? Why hadn't she checked who was knocking on the door of her bedroom? Why had fate allowed her to be trapped in this untenable situation? Her heart was hammering into her ribs, tingles of awareness shooting to every part of her body from the pressure of Raphael's hand on her waist.

'From the span of my hand against the curve of your waist I can tell that your waist can't be much more than twenty-two inches,' he announced matter-of-factly.

A swift spasm of shocked recognition at his accuracy shook Charley's body—or was it the fact that Raphael's fingertip was moving in a straight line down over her still tensed stomach, causing rivulets of unwanted sensation to run from his touch with faster gathering force the lower his fingertip moved. Like lava from a long-suppressed volcano, they gathered speed and spread out, overwhelming the opposition of her tightened muscles and sending their message of aching arousal deep into her body. Surely it was only her own wanton imagination that was telling her that he had momentarily flattened the whole of his hand against her body, so that the heel of his palm momentarily pressed hard against the vulnerable flesh surmounting her sex? Shame, guilt and fear surged through her. How pitiful she was for actually thinking what she was thinking. She could understand why her body would be aroused by Raphael's touch, but how on earth could she imagine that he might want her?

Raphael was now drawing a line out to her hip

bone and telling her coolly, 'Your hip measurement is approximately thirty-four inches.'

'Thirty-four and a half, actually.' Charley managed to find the courage to correct him.

'Which is still too narrow for your height.'

'Which you can also assess, no doubt?' Charley couldn't stop herself from snapping.

'Certainly,' Raphael agreed, releasing her arm to step close to her and turn her round, holding her against his own body and directing her attention to the full-length mirror in front of her.

'I am six foot three, which means that you are around five foot nine—and you have long legs, in proportion to your height.' His hand brushed the top of her bare thigh, causing her to grit her teeth to control the shudder that gripped her.

Charley was beyond telling him that in fact she was five nine and a quarter. She was beyond doing anything other than staring with growing horror at the sharp peaking of her nipples beneath her thin top, the erotic contrast between their erect, eager stiffness and the swell and softness of her breasts filling her with humiliation.

'What I cannot understand,' Raphael continued as she battled to force herself to concentrate on what he was saying and not what his touch was doing to her, 'is why a woman—any woman—should want to conceal the beauty of the perfect form that nature has bestowed upon her with such ugly, concealing clothes.'

Distracted from her humiliation by the unexpectedness of his words, Charley struggled to assimilate them. Raphael was praising her body? Describing it as perfect? The body she had always felt so inferior? Her heart thudded against her ribs, making her dizzy with emotion. But wasn't it more likely that he had simply meant that the female form in general was beautiful and perfect, rather than meaning her body in particular?

Shakily, Charley tried to pull herself away from him and turn round at the same time, but somehow all she managed to do was turn so that now she was face to face as well as body to body with Raphael, whilst his hands still held her hips. Automatically she looked up at him, her ability to breathe stifled by the way his probing gaze fastened on her mouth and stayed there. Immediately, as though commanded to do so, her lips parted, her breath coming quickly and urgently, lifting her chest in small unsteady movements. What would she do if he kissed her? She could feel his hands tightening against her body. What would it feel like to have them caressing her? Her whole body jolted as though it had received an electric shock so strong was its reaction to her own thoughts. She wanted to lean into him and offer herself to him. She wanted to curl her hand behind his head and bring his mouth down to her own. She wanted to feel his touch against her bare skin… She wanted…

Abruptly Raphael released her, and stepped back from her, leaving Charley to tell herself that she was glad that he had brought an end to her reckless and unwanted imaginings.

'Very well, then,' she told him, struggling for normality. 'I'll wear the jeans, but that's all. I don't need the jacket.'

Raphael had stepped into the shadow of the window and she couldn't see his expression properly.

'It is over two hundred years since the garden fell into disrepair,' he told her coolly. 'Many parts of it are thick with overgrown plants. You will need the jacket to protect you from thorns. Now, I shall expect you to be downstairs and ready to accompany me to the garden in one hour's time. Is that understood?'

Reluctantly Charley nodded her head.

As he walked down the corridor from Charlotte's bedroom there was only one image in Raphael's head, and one thought on his mind. The trouble was that the image and the thought were at war with one another. The image was that of Charlotte standing looking at him with defiant pride, her breasts rising and falling with the force of her emotions, her long legs going on for ever, making him ache to have them wrapped around his own body as the two of them lay together on the bed, her naked flesh warm and soft to his touch, her hands on his body, her mouth opening to his as he gave in to the aching need of his desire for her—a desire that in his imagination she shared and matched. He had never wanted a woman so much nor so illogically. Logically there was nothing about her that should have appealed to him—not physically, nor mentally, nor in any other way. His taste ran to soignée, elegant and mature women in their thirties, like him—women of the world, not fiercely passionate young women who dressed in ill-fitting clothes and upset and undermined a project of great personal importance to him. His mind told him that he should not want her, but his body told him equally powerfully that it did. In this instance, with something as important to him as the renovation of the garden at stake, it was what his mind was telling him that mattered, and it was on what his mind was telling him that he intended to focus.

Charley walked slowly over to the mirror and studied her reflection. Tentatively she touched her waist, and then, driven by an impulse she couldn't control, she pulled off her clothes. She couldn't remember the last time she had looked at her own naked body. How would she, when she normally avoided looking at it? It must be the sunlight that was giving her skin that soft glow, that sheen that said it wanted to be touched and admired. She lifted her own hand to her body, touching it as and where Raphael had done, trying to see it with his eyes, and then tensing. What was she doing? Wasn't the situation difficult enough for her already, without her adding even more potential discomfort to it?

She looked at the bedroom door, reminding herself that she didn't have much time to get downstairs if she was to keep to the schedule Raphael had given her.

Ten minutes later Charley looked down at the jeans she was wearing. They were a perfect fit—a far better fit and a far better cut than the ones she had been wearing, their slim shape emphasising the length of her legs and clinging to her hips.

She was also wearing the new tee shirt and the leather jacket, its fabric soft against her fingertips. When she'd looked at herself in the bedroom's full-length mirror she'd been caught off guard by the difference the new clothes made to her appearance. Even the hair clouding round her face looked different. Her reflection was more feminine somehow—but of course that was impossible. She was seeing what she wanted to see because of the way she felt about Raphael. Because, foolishly and dangerously, she wanted him.

Angry with herself, she used the dark brown ribbon that had been wrapped round the tissue-folded clothes to tie back her hair. She couldn't stay up here any longer. If she did Raphael might come and look for her—or was that what she secretly wanted? No! Grabbing her shoulder bag, she headed for the door.

Almost the second she stepped off the final marble stair and into the hallway the door to Raphael's office opened and he came out, acknowledging her presence with the briefest nod before heading for the open double doors through which the sunlight was streaming.

What had she been expecting? Charley asked herself as she lengthened her own stride to follow him. That he would make a comment about the way she looked? A flattering comment? She was far too sensible for that kind of silliness, and the slightly leaden feeling inside her chest cavity was not disappointment, but merely the effect of eating a cold croissant, Charley told herself firmly.

Raphael had already reached the Ferrari, and was holding open the passenger door for her, closing it firmly once she was in the passen-

ger seat without having looked directly at her
or even spoken to her.

She felt the car depress slightly as Raphael
got in and started up the engine. The warmth
of the sun had released the scent of the
leather interior, along with a more subtle
scent which her senses recognised as belonging to Raphael.

It didn't take them long to reach the outskirts of the town. The ruins of a medieval
castle and its curtain wall, the ancient stone
painted soft rose by the sun as they approached
it across a flat agricultural plain filled with
crops and livestock, were etched against the
skyline. A single tower, ruined and roofless,
pointed up towards the clouds.

'What happened to the castle?' Charley
couldn't resist asking Raphael.

'It and the town were attacked and put under
siege by a more powerful force than my
ancestor had at his command. Fortunately he
had friends who came to his aid and drove the
attackers back, saving the town and the lives of

my ancestors, but not the castle. It was as a result of that attack that the then duke decided to build a new home for himself, away from the town.'

Charley nodded her head as they drove into the town through an arched gateway in the medieval wall.

Ancient buildings leaned into one another as though for support on either side of the narrow cobbled street, and splashes of sunshine where it was intersected by another street turned the paving soft gold. High above their heads Charley could see lines of washing, and here and there a heavy wooden door was open to reveal a glimpse of a private courtyard basking in the sunlight.

She could smell fresh-baked bread, olive oil and herbs coming from the baskets of a group of elderly women dressed in black with faces seamed like walnuts, standing talking outside what was obviously a bakers, and then they were out of the narrow street and in the town square—the Piazza Grande.

In the centre of the square was an ornate fountain, and opposite the town hall there was what was obviously a market area, although there were no stalls on it today, so that she had a clear view of the pedestal topped by a life-size statue of an eagle.

'The eagle is part of our family emblem,' Raphael told her, following the direction of her glance. 'There is a legend that our land here in Tuscany was originally given to a Roman legionnaire who fought for Caesar and saved his life. This ancestor then adopted the Imperial Eagle from his legion's standard into his personal arms.'

Charley tried not to look as entranced as she felt. Imagine having that kind of lore as part of your personal family history. Had the mother Raphael had lost taken him on her lap and told him stories about his family's past? An ache of sadness filled her as she thought of her own childhood. It had been such a terrible time for them all when their parents had died—especially when they had learned that the lovely vicarage in which they had been brought up was heavily mortgaged, and that their parents had no savings nor any life insurance which might have eased their orphaned daughters' financial position.

The traffic had cleared and they were now travelling down another narrow street, and then through another archway in the town's wall. Charley gripped the sides of her seat as Raphael changed gear and the sports car surged forward.

The hard look he gave her derided her timidity as he told her, 'I don't know what kind of men you normally share a car with, but I can assure you that I am not the kind of driver who over-estimates his skill or takes foolish risks.'

'I'm not used to such a powerful car.' Or such a powerful man? Charley looked away from Raphael's face, only to realise that her gaze was slipping helplessly over the tanned flesh to his wrist as he manoeuvred the gear lever. Her foolish imagination was painting vivid images inside her head of Raphael's hand on her body. A surge of self-conscious heat burned through her. Why was he able to have such an effect on her? It had never happened before with any other man, and she didn't want it happening now. She could all too easily picture the mixture of arrogant disdain and mockery with which he would look at her if he knew what she was feeling. Her, a clumsy, un-feminine woman, untutored in the arts of feminine seduction, ill equipped to please a man of his undoubted experience? He would no doubt reject her desire for him with haughty contempt.

She had been so preoccupied with her own thoughts that it took her several seconds to realise that the car was slowing down and they had reached the entrance to the garden.

Charley looked at the dilapidated double colonnade that marked the entrance. Most of its columns were either missing or damaged, and over the top of it there was a tangle of overgrown wild vines on which the leaves were just beginning to open in the spring sunshine.

Silently Charley got out of the Ferrari when Raphael opened the door for her. Now, having seen the original drawings, she could well understand why Raphael wanted to see the garden restored to its original glory.

'This way,' Raphael instructed, producing the key to unlock the bolts that secured the heavy wood doors.

CHAPTER FIVE

CHARLEY had seen the garden before, of course, but then Raphael hadn't been with her, she acknowledged nearly two hours later. She stood almost knee-deep in a tangle of under-growth and weeds in the middle of what, according to the original plans, had once been a beautiful parterre garden, with neatly clipped borders and central features of cherubs playing musical instruments mounted on classically inspired plinths.

Standing here, in the middle of this ruined paradise, Charley was filled with sadness for the loss of so much beauty, and a yearning to do everything she could to restore it to what it should have been.

'There was a fountain here, according to the original designs, connected to the ornamental lake by a system of formal waterways and canals. If I remember correctly, your renovations called for the lake to be filled in.'

Raphael's comment brought her back to reality.

'It's filled with rubbish and leaking. It would cost nearly as much again as the town council had allowed for the entire renovation just to restore the lake and to put in the safeguards that modern laws demand,' she pointed out.

'It is my wish that everything will now be restored to match the original design—and that includes the lake.'

Raphael heard Charley sigh, and saw her look across the tangled mass of overgrowth and damaged masonry in the direction of the lake, now hidden from view.

'You do not agree with me, I take it?' Raphael demanded.

Charley turned towards him in astonishment.

'On the contrary—I can't think of anything

that would be more rewarding than to see this place become once again what it was. It's a project anyone would give their eye teeth to be involved in…bringing to life something so wonderful.' Emotional tears momentarily blurred Charley's vision, as her feelings got the better of her. 'The people of the town are fortunate to have you to do something so generous, and I…I feel that I am fortunate too, to be a part of such a project,' she admitted.

Now it was Raphael's turn to look away from her. Her honesty surprised him. He hadn't been expecting it, and nor had he been expecting her open emotional reaction to the garden. Perhaps, after all, he did have the right person to manage the project—a person who had just shown him that she was capable of being touched to the deepest part of herself by what had once been and what was now lost. Such a person would give everything she had to give to a project that engaged her emotions. And to the man who engaged them as well?

Charlotte Wareham's sexual passions were

hers to give to whomsoever she chose and no concern of his, Raphael reminded himself. It was as a project manager that he was interested in her, and not as a bedmate.

'If you're serious about the lake—' Charley began, breaking into the silence.

'I am.'

'My guess is that the restoration work will require the advice of proper experts who have experience in that kind of work. There is a team booked to come in and start clearing all the mess away, but I don't think they will be the right people to deal with the lake. It might be best to get in touch with… Well, in England I'd probably try English Heritage or the National Trust. Any organisation with artistic appreciation, that believes in the importance of preserving the heritage we've been left by artists of the past, couldn't help but want to be part of a project like this one. It would have been a dream come true for me when I was studying Fine Art.'

She was intelligent, and proactive, but above

all her passion for the project was so strong that it shone from her eyes and could be heard in her voice. Why on earth would a woman who felt as she so obviously did give up her Fine Arts degree to study accountancy, and then take a job that involved her in projects calling for the appalling replicas he had seen her with? Raphael wondered, his probing mind curious against his better judgement. There was something here that didn't add up. His curiosity aroused, Raphael decided to put his suspicions to the test.

'Feeling as you so obviously do, it must have been hard for you to give up your Fine Arts course?' he began, deliberately making his question sound casual.

Still wrapped in the emotions the garden had evoked, and in the understanding and harmony they had shared, Charley forgot to be on her guard, and responded without thinking.

'Yes, it was.'

She was shocked back to reality when Raphael asked, 'Then why did you?'

His question made her suddenly aware of the foolish relaxation of her guard, and she was doubly a fool for having let him see just how much the garden had affected her.

'You don't answer? Why not, I wonder? Is it perhaps because there is something you wish to hide? Perhaps it was not so much that you decided to change to another course, but that you were requested to do so by your tutors.'

Stung by Raphael's subtle allegation that she had had to drop her course because she had not been good enough, Charley told him fiercely, 'No. It was nothing like that.'

'Then what *was* it like? You are in effect now working under my command. I have a right to ask this question and to receive a truthful answer,' Raphael pressed.

Charley lifted her hands in a gesture of defeat.

'Very well then. If you must know, I applied for the course without telling my family what I was going to be studying. They thought… That is to say I really wanted to do an arts degree and study Fine Arts, but I knew my father would laugh at me, and say that I was far too much of a clumsy tomboy to be allowed anywhere near fine art. My sisters are both so pretty, and so feminine; I am the plain, awkward one of the family. I knew that for my own sake my father would try to persuade me to study something else—something more practical.'

Charley gave a small sigh, whilst Raphael digested her words in silence. He would certainly not have described Charley as either awkward or plain. It was true that hers was not the chocolate box variety of 'pretty', but in Raphael's estimation Charley possessed something far more potent. His body certainly thought so, from the way it responded to the delicate air of hidden sensuality she carried with her.

'But I was offered the course so they let me do it. I was less than a year into it when our parents were killed. Then we found out there was no money and that the house, our childhood home, was heavily mortgaged and would have to be sold. Lizzie, my elder sister, was working in London at the time for a top-notch interior designer, and then Ruby told us that she was pregnant. She was only seventeen. Lizzie and I both felt so guilty; she was practically still a baby herself. We had to do something. We couldn't just abandon Ruby and her babies as the babies' father had, so Lizzie moved back to Cheshire and set up her own small business, and…'

'And you decided to sacrifice your own plans in order to earn money to help support your family?'

'It wasn't a sacrifice,' Charley protested immediately. 'We wanted to stay together and support one another.'

'Maybe it wasn't a sacrifice then, but I think you feel that it is now,' Raphael corrected her. 'I think that now, here in Italy, you have become aware of all you have denied yourself.'

Charley couldn't look at him. Was it just her plans to take a Fine Arts degree and all that went with it to which he was referring? Or had he guessed about the other things she had denied herself—things like being free to be herself, and not the family tomboy, to explore and enjoy her sexuality as that self? She hoped not. That would be too humiliating for her to bear.

'Being in Italy has made me realise how much I would have enjoyed studying art,' she admitted in a stifled voice, unable to look at him as she did so. 'And of course the recession has changed things. Before it happened I told myself that if my job got too unbearable I could always leave and find another one, and that maybe one day I'd get the opportunity to study and travel, but now of course that's impossible. I do wish—' She stopped and shook her head. 'There's no point in talking about what one can't have, and I am very grateful to you for giving me the opportunity to work on something so very special.'

Inwardly Charley cursed herself. She had done it again—admitting that she was grateful to him, humbling and even humiliating herself, making herself far too vulnerable by her tacit admission that she so desperately wanted to be part of the renovation project. Maybe so, but at least she had been true to herself and to her own code, Charley comforted herself. She couldn't pretend that she had no wish to be involved in the project to renovate the garden when the exact opposite was the case.

Raphael turned away from Charley, not wanting her to see in his expression the feelings he didn't even want to acknowledge to himself. Her speech, her gratitude, the fact that her emotions about the garden were so in accord with his own, had rubbed against a vulnerable place within himself—a wound only half healed that he had believed until now was fully healed. Beneath the thin skin that covered that wound lay emotions and regrets so painful and dark that he could not bear to admit they were there. A whole adult lifetime dedicated to pretending that such a wound did not exist was now in danger of being ripped aside to reveal the truth. But that truth could not be acknowledged. He must adhere to the course he had set himself. He must not waver. Inwardly Raphael cursed Charley for the effect she was having on him, and damned himself for even thinking of weakening.

Raphael's silence made Charley feel anxious. Something had changed. She could almost feel the coldness now emanating from him, replacing what had previously been close to a shared openness about the importance of the garden. Now that was gone, and when Raphael swung back towards her, his expression shielded by the shadows, his voice was hard with warning as he told her, 'According to your project notes, you've allowed three months for clearing the site.'

Charley nodded her head.

'I want to see that work done in two months, not three.'

'That can't be done,' Charley protested. The intimacy they had shared earlier was over, she recognised, and Raphael was once again a man who was making it plain exactly how he felt about her and her ability to do the job he would no doubt have preferred to give to someone else.

'Anything can be done if one goes about it in the right way.' And that included finding a way to stop his senses from being so aware of her and his body from aching for her, Raphael reminded himself inwardly. 'As I have already told you,' he informed Charley, 'I expect my orders to be followed and carried out. There is no room on this project for a project manager who cannot achieve what needs to be achieved. If you feel you cannot do that…'

He was challenging her—setting her targets that could not be achieved because he wanted to get rid of her.

Well, she would show him.

'Very well,' she told him. 'But it will be expensive.' Now she was the one challenging him—to pay up or back down.

'Half as much again as you have already allowed for the cost of bringing in the extra manpower, but worth it for what it will save in time,' Raphael agreed with a dismissive shrug, before adding warningly, 'However, what is in question is not whether or not I am prepared to incur additional costs where I think it necessary but whether—or not—you are up to the task of managing this project.'

Charley had had enough. What had happened to their earlier harmony and the belief she had had then that he was prepared to give her a chance? They shared a recognition of just what the garden must once have been. Or had she just imagined it? Because she had wanted to connect emotionally with him? Charley's heart thudded into her ribs. That was nonsense. He meant nothing to her. It was the job that was important. Nothing else.

Was it? So why was she feeling so hurt and rejected, so sharply reminded of the way she had so often felt as a child, when her parents had compared her looks unfavourably to those of her sisters, making her aware that she was not good enough and that they wished that she was different—just as Raphael obviously didn't feel that she was good enough, and wished that the project was being managed by someone else.

It was such a blow after the intimacy and understanding she felt they had shared that Charley couldn't stop herself from bursting out, 'You want to get rid of me, don't you? You want me to fail. You want to bully me into saying I can't cope, just as my boss wants to bully me into handing in my resignation so that he can give my job to his daughter. Well, much as I'd love to oblige you both, and set myself free from the necessity of having to put up with you, I can't and I won't. I need this job, and I need it because, as I have already told you, without the money I earn from it my sisters and I could lose our home. Because of that I will manage this project successfully—no matter how hard you try to push me into leaving.'

Raphael turned away from her again. He was loath to admit it, but there was an element of truth in her accusation that he wanted to get rid of her. And not just because he doubted her ability to handle the project successfully. No, it was the effect she was having on him physically as a man that was the prime cause of his desire to get her out of his life. Raphael wasn't used to his body, his senses, challenging the rules he had made for the way he lived his life. The reality was that they had never done so before, and certainly not to the extent they were now—invading his thoughts and his judgement with their increasingly intense demands.

'There are other jobs,' he told Charley unsympathetically.

Charley looked at him in disbelief, and then shook her head.

'I don't know what world you live in,' she told him scornfully, 'but it isn't the real world. There's a recession on—but of course that won't affect people like you. Thousands of people are out of work, and thousands more— of which I am one—are living in fear of losing their job. If that wasn't the case do you think I would stay in this one?'

Now she had done it, Charley thought miserably, her anger giving way to anxiety as she recognised how outspoken she had been.

'I can manage this project successfully,' she told Raphael. 'And I *will* manage it successfully.'

The earlier harmony she had felt they shared had been nothing more than an illusion, Charley told herself bitterly—a trick and a trap into which she had fallen by allowing Raphael to get under her guard. Too late to regret now the information she had given him about herself; too late to tell herself that she should never have listened to her senses and her body instead of her head, when they had whispered excitedly to her of their reaction to Raphael. Her head knew perfectly well that there could be no intimacy—of any kind—between her and Raphael, no matter what her foolish senses might have wanted to believe. All she could do was make sure that she didn't make the same mistake again.

The garden covered several acres, and there were parts of it—like the part they were in now—that Charley hadn't seen on her earlier visit because access to them was so overgrown.

Striding ahead of her, Raphael had come to a halt outside the ruins of what had once been a pretty garden temple.

'Down here there is something I particularly want to discuss with you,' he told her, indicating a set of steps that led downwards to a heavy wooden door. 'But take care on the steps—they are damaged and slippery.'

Charley hesitated. She didn't like underground places—never had done since she had been accidentally locked in the vicarage's cellar as a child. But she knew she couldn't refuse without making a fool of herself and showing a vulnerability she did not want Raphael to see, so she followed Raphael down the stone steps, trying to control her reluctance and anxiety as he unlocked the door.

Just the sound of it creaking back on its hinges when Raphael pushed it open was enough to increase Charley's apprehension.

'Down here is the chamber containing the mechanism for the fountains. I've had someone looking at it, and it's still working, although the fountains and sprinklers themselves need repairing and restoring. Once they are in working order again they should prove a tremendous draw for visitors. One of the things I want to do—the only modernisation of the gardens I will permit—is the addition of lighting. The cabling for that will need to be put in at an early stage, and you will need to make arrangements for that.'

Charley nodded her head. He was quite right that specially designed lighting would enhance the garden.

'It is my intention that the money brought in via future visitors to the garden will go directly to the town, for the benefit of its people—especially the young people, to provide them with the opportunity to learn new skills. There is no industry here, no work for the young, and without them the town will eventually die.'

His altruistic plans surprised Charley. They seemed at odds with her own judgement of him—or was it just *her* he felt didn't deserve to earn a living?

Charley was just about to respond when she saw a small shadow flit past her out of the corner of her eye, followed by another.

'What…?' she began anxiously, but Raphael anticipated her.

'It is nothing to worry about,' he told her casually. 'It is only bats. They have made a home here. If you come down here and look closely you can see them hanging up in the roof. We've obviously disturbed them.'

Look closely? Charley shook her head, and then whirled round as another bat flew past her, losing her balance on the crumbling stone as she did so.

Raphael must have moved quickly, because he had been several feet away from her when she had slipped and now he was holding her.

The bats were forgotten. All Charley could think about was her proximity to Raphael. Her heart was thudding into her ribs with a mixture of forbidden excitement and longing. She must not feel like this, she warned herself.

She must not raise her head and look at him. She must not let her gaze rest yearningly on his mouth. She must not let her heart thud with anticipation and longing whilst she looked up into his eyes, her own eyes telling him what she most wanted.

She must not, but she was.

This was not what he should be doing, Raphael knew, but his hard grip on Charley's upper arms still softened into a hold that was more a caress, the pads of his fingertips smoothing the soft leather against her skin. He could see the pulse beating frantically in her throat, inciting him to capture it with his lips and then trace his way up to her mouth. He'd already lifted his hand, preparatory to cupping her face so that he could hold her still beneath his kiss. What harm would one kiss do? At least then he would know.

Know what? That he wanted her? He didn't need to kiss her to discover that.

Raphael was going to kiss her! Charley leaned helplessly towards him, and then stopped when he released her abruptly, almost thrusting her away from him.

'I thought you said that your leg was fine,' he said angrily. 'If you are still having a problem with it you should have said so. The last thing I want is to have—'

'To carry me out of here?' Charley stopped him. She was shamefully close to tears, foolishly hurt by his anger and his lack of understanding. 'Well, you needn't worry. There's nothing wrong with my leg. The bats made me stumble, that's all.'

Carry her? The savage surge of physical reaction hardening his body at the thought of holding her in his arms increased Raphael's fury—not against Charley but against himself. He could feel it burning through him, beating at the defences of his self-control: anger against himself for not recognising that she might be in pain; anger against himself for wanting her; anger against the strictures placed upon him because of what and who he was, forbidding him from living as other men did. Anger, but not rage. Not that feeling he had sworn he would never allow to possess him ever again—that wall of savagery that had once risen up inside him, sweeping over him like a red mist, obliterating reason and humanity, possessing him with its violence, forcing him to accept the cursed reality of what he had inherited, the reality of what he was.

That feeling, experienced once and never forgotten by him, was his dark shadow—always with him, always reminding him, a warning of what might lie ahead of him in his future if it wasn't controlled. And who could say that it always would be? Who could say that it wouldn't grow and take over like some progressive disease? Like the form of madness that it was? So that he ended up not only risking passing on his own tainted inheritance to a future generation but also, in the grip of his own madness, destroying those he should most protect.

Images he had kept locked away burst past

the doors he had closed against them. His mother's pretty sitting room, its air carrying her scent, the sunlight falling on the petit point that was her favourite hobby laid down on a small table, the chair on which she always sat whilst doing it beside the table.

Like a film inside his head Raphael could see himself reaching for that chair in a fit of anger—of madness—and then hurling it against the marble fireplace with such force that it had lain broken and splintered, its red silk seat covering resembling a pool of blood against the white marble.

No! The denial, silent and agonising, was wrung from deep inside of him, but Raphael knew that no amount of regret could take back what he had done in the savagery of his rage against his mother—the person who had loved him so very much and who had least deserved that rage. For the rest of his life he must be on his guard against that rage—against that madness ever possessing him again—and that meant controlling his emotions, not allowing himself to get close emotionally to anyone—for their own sake and protection.

CHAPTER SIX

IT WAS no use. She could mentally castigate herself as much as she liked for being too vulnerable to her emotions when she should have been listening to her head. Raphael was not someone she could afford to let her guard down around, Charley warned herself as she paused in front of the portraits of Raphael's parents— painted just after their marriage, so Anna had told her when she had asked about them.

She looked up at the portrait of Raphael's mother, dark-haired like her son, and dark-eyed like the husband whose portrait she was turning towards. What had struck Charley the first time she had seen the portraits was the shining happiness in Raphael's mother's eyes as she looked towards her husband, and the tenderness with which he looked back at her.

They had been very much in love, Anna had told her, the young Duchess having fallen in love with the twenty-two-year-old Duke at her own fourteenth birthday party, swearing that she would marry no one else. Witnessing now that look of shining love, and knowing of the grief that had driven her to take her own life after her husband's death, touched Charley's own emotions. Poor lady. And poor Raphael too? After all, he had lost his parents as she had lost hers, and at a much younger and more vulnerable age. She shrugged the thought away. She did not want to feel sorry for Raphael. She did not want to feel anything for him at all. Charley's heart started to beat unsteadily as she tried to deny what her body was telling her—that it was already too late for her to tell herself that.

She had spent the morning exchanging e-mails with the contractors who were to clear the site. It had taken some hard bargaining on her part to secure their agreement to do the extra work in the timescale Raphael had stipulated, and at a cost that was not excessive. She had also sourced three contenders for the lighting Raphael wanted installed, sending them copies of the original plans and asking for their suggestions for effective lighting and projected costs.

Raphael had sent for her, and no doubt he would want to know exactly how much progress she had made. Apprehensively and reluctantly, Charley knocked on the door to Raphael's office and then pushed it open.

'You wanted to see me?'

'Yes,' Raphael confirmed. 'I've been in touch with someone I know in Florence—a member of a committee responsible for the maintenance of some of the city's most historic buildings. He has supplied me with the contact details for both a landscape architect and the head of Florence's most prestigious academy for craftsmen. Men and women who study there learn the skills of traditional arts. My contact tells me that this is where we will find the very best sculptors to recreate the garden's ornaments. First, though, we shall need to convince Niccolo Volpari, who runs the school, that our project is worthy of his students.'

'That sounds excellent. If you give me his e-mail address I'll get in touch with him and arrange for him to come out and see the garden.'

Raphael shook his head.

'This is a very important and a very busy man. We will have to go to Florence to see him, not the other way around. The decision as to whether or not he will accept us onto his list of clients will be his and not ours,' he repeated. 'It is from the academy that the city of Florence finds sculptors and painters, gilders and carvers, stonemasons and master builders when any restoration work needs to be undertaken. It is Niccolo's teachers who will examine what is left of the garden's ornaments and then recommend the pupil who will replicate the damaged pieces.'

Raphael got up from behind his desk and walked towards the window. Charley watched him, her glance clinging to the broad span of his shoulders and the way his body tapered down to his hips. His shirt, which was no doubt handmade and expensive, somehow delineated the male shape of his body without in any way clinging to it as her avid gaze was doing. Why was it that Italian men, or at least this Italian man, seemed able to wear a pair of chinos in a way that focused female attention on the powerful muscles in his thighs? The way his muscles moved when he moved filled her female mind with mental images of hard-muscled flesh, and the power it contained, its maleness emphasised by the dark silkiness of body hair.

Charley dragged her gaze away, panicking when it wanted to linger, as she heard Raphael speaking.

'Niccolo Volpari is insisting on seeing both of us. He is known for his eccentricity, apparently, where the projects he takes on are concerned, and I am told by those with whom he works that it would not do to refuse.'

And he had wanted to refuse, Raphael acknowledged—all the more so when he had discovered that members of a convention of Michelangelo admirers from all over the world were currently filling virtually every hotel bedroom in Florence.

'Unfortunately the only time he can see us is for dinner tomorrow evening, which means that we shall have to stay in Florence overnight—Italians do not eat until late in the evening.'

Unfortunately? Charley couldn't think of anything she'd rather do than have the chance to spend time in Florence. She might even be able to snatch enough time to visit its famous market and buy herself an inexpensive change of clothes to supplement the jeans and jacket Raphael had given her and her two tee shirts.

'We shall stay overnight in my Florence apartment.'

Now her excitement had become a complex

mix of emotions, some of which were far too dangerous for her to want to question.

'We will leave first thing tomorrow morning. I warn you that my contact tells me that Niccolo Volpari does not suffer fools gladly, and he will have many questions he wants to ask, many tests the project will have to pass before he is satisfied and prepared to recommend that his artistes work on it. Their work is the best of the best, and he boasts that Michelangelo himself would not be able to tell the difference between his own *David* and a copy made by Volpari students. Now, what progress have you made with regard to the restoration of the lake?'

'I've been in touch with English Heritage and the National Trust, and they have given me the names of three Italian-based organisations that have the know-how to take on the project. I've e-mailed all three of them, but as yet I have not received a response. I've also informed the company clearing the site that you now want the work done in two months, and they have agreed to supply an extra team to ensure that that target is met. It will mean floodlighting the whole area, which will add to the cost, and paying overtime. I've got the figures here. I wanted to get your approval of them before I give them the go-ahead.'

Raphael reached the desk just as Charley was placing the papers on it. One of the papers slipped, and as she retrieved it somehow her knuckles inadvertently brushed against the soft fabric stretched against Raphael's thigh. The shock of sensation that burned through her was such that Charley immediately released the papers and withdrew her hand, not daring to look at Raphael, her whole body burning up with discomfort. Why on earth was she behaving like such a gauche fool? Her touch had been accidental, probably not even felt by Raphael, and yet here she was, behaving like a virgin who had found her hand resting un-expectedly on a full-on male erection, instead of an adult woman whose hand had merely brushed accidentally against a piece of fabric.

'I'm always so clumsy,' she heard herself saying apologetically. 'My parents were always telling me that.'

She started to bend down, to retrieve the piece of paper that was now on the floor, but Raphael stopped her, his voice harsh as he instructed, 'No, leave it. I'll look at it later. Right now I have some estate business to deal with, and some phone calls to make, and I am sure that you have work to do also.'

Hot-cheeked, Charley nodded her head and quickly made her escape from his office.

Raphael waited until Charley had gone before he bent down to retrieve the fallen piece of paper, his knuckles showing white through the tan on his skin as he did so. Had he allowed Charley to kneel down and retrieve the paper, as she had plainly intended to do, she would have seen quite plainly his arousal and known the cause of it. What manner of man was he that the mere accidental touch of a woman he desired was enough to breach the defences of his self-control?

Back in her room, Charley tried to concentrate on her work, knowing even as she did so that concentrating on anything other than the fool she had just made of herself was going to be impossible. Inside her head were images of Raphael: the way he stood, the way he moved, the way her imagination stripped the clothes from his body, the way her whole body had trembled when she had touched him. Charley gave a small groan of defeat. Thinking about work was impossible now that she had unleashed the dangerously sensual awareness of Raphael that was building inside her—wildly reckless and foolish thoughts of an intimacy between them that could never happen and that she should not even *want* to happen. But her body did want it to happen, and every day it wanted it to happen a little more. A little more? Didn't she mean an awful lot more? Charley questioned herself. She was like a girl in the grip of an impossible sexual crush on an idol, not a woman who ought to know better. Beneath her tee shirt her nipples peaked and ached on the surge of sexual longing that rushed through her.

Charley groaned again. She must not feel like this. She must not!

CHAPTER SEVEN

FLORENCE and Raphael! Florence with Raphael! Was she really sure that was a good idea? Charley asked herself. But then did she really have any choice? A shiver, half expectation, half dread, but wholly sensual, stroked taunting fingertips down her spine, immediately sending into disarray all the promises she had made herself the previous day about stopping herself from thinking about the effect he had on her sexually. Couldn't her body understand how humiliating it was for her to want a man who had made it plain how little time he had for her? Raphael did not want her in his life in any capacity at all, and he most certainly did not want her in his bed. Her breath caught on a savagely sweet ache of longing, which she had to fight to suppress. Why should Raphael want a woman like her—a woman devoid of beauty and female grace, a woman devoid of sexual expertise and sensual allure? He didn't, and he wouldn't, and if she had any self-respect she would find a way to stop herself from reacting to him in a way that could easily end up with her making a total fool of herself if she ever accidentally betrayed to Raphael himself what had happened to her.

What she should be doing was focusing on the job she had to do.

It wasn't even as though she could blame Raphael for the way she felt, or claim that he was the one who had deliberately made her feel the way she did. The truth was the opposite. Charley had grown up being honest with herself—especially when it came to her own shortcomings and failures. She couldn't blame Raphael for the fact that she was so acutely and intensely susceptible to him. The responsibility for that lay with her, and within her. But it wasn't too late for her to change things. She could draw a line under her vulnerability to him and set herself some new conditions and rules for the way she would permit herself to react to him. First and foremost amongst those rules would be at all times observing a proper professional attitude towards him, maintaining a proper professional distance between them. She could do it. She must do it, Charley told herself as she made her way downstairs. After all she had texted her sisters now, to tell them that she would be staying on in Italy to begin immediate work on the garden restoration, so it was too late to change her mind.

There was no sign of Raphael in the hallway, so whilst she waited for him Charley was free to study the frescoes in more detail, marvelling at the skill of the artist who had painted them. Every expression told its own story about the character who wore it, but it was the expressions on the faces of the three children grouped together that drew Charley. The tallest of them, a boy obviously meant to represent the young heir, had all of Raphael's arrogance and pride in his expression as he stood slightly in front of his mother and brother and sister, his clothes richer than theirs, his gaze fixed on the distant landscape, as though aware that one day those lands would belong to him. To his side, his sister, in her ermine-trimmed gown, was looking to her mother for approval as an envoy dressed in livery kneeled before her, offering her a roll of parchment on a shield—perhaps meant to signify a marriage agreement? Charley wondered. The youngest child, another boy, was seated on his mother's lap, reaching for the gold cross she was wearing. As a second son he might well have been destined for high office in the church, Charlotte recognised.

'The third Duchess with her children.'

The sound of Raphael's voice sent a frisson of forbidden pleasure curling down Charley's spine. Not trusting herself to turn round, she told him, 'The eldest son looks a little like you.'

'He was killed when the castle came under attack from enemy forces. He died defending his mother and his sister.'

Charley shivered. Raphael's words showed her that despite the air of arrogance and superiority the boy carried with him, underneath it he had still been vulnerable. Unlike Raphael, who she was sure would never be vulnerable to anything or anyone.

'You are ready to leave?'

Charley nodded her head, wondering as she followed him out to the waiting Ferrari what had caused the swift frowning look Raphael had given her.

It had rained in the night, and the morning sunshine was filling the air with the rich scent of damp earth and growing things—of life returning to the world after the darkness of winter.

At least now there was no need for her to feel deprived because her stay in Italy would be too brief for her to see all those things she longed to see, Charley told herself. There would be ample time for her to visit its cities and its art galleries, to breathe in its magic and fill her senses with its beauty.

The Ferrari made nothing of the kilometres, each signpost promising that they were getting closer to Florence.

'We shall go first to my apartment,' Raphael announced, 'since we shall be staying there.'

Charley's heart rolled over inside her chest. She didn't trust herself to say anything, but then what could she say? *I don't want to stay in your apartment because I want you and I'm afraid of betraying that to you?* Hardly.

The sound of Raphael's voice cut across her uncomfortable thoughts, giving her a welcome excuse not to dwell on them.

'This evening, as you know, we shall be dining with Niccolo Volpari, Antonio Riccardi, the landscape architect, and their wives.' Another frowningly assessing look, just like the one he had given her earlier when they had left the *palazzo,* raked her from head to toe, leaving her feeling vulnerable but reluctant to demand an explanation.

They had reached the outskirts of the city and were turning off the autostrada, heading for the River Arno.

'The Ponte Vecchio is to your left, beyond the Ponte alle Grazia,' Raphael informed her, as though guessing what was on her mind as they reached the river.

It made Charley feel dizzy to think of the history that lay before her, like a precious jewel waiting to be admired. Now Raphael was driving through a maze of narrow streets with names straight from history, bordered by buildings that had Charley silent with awe. In a small square she saw a sign for the Piazza della Signoria and the Uffizi, and her heart leapt with excitement. People, many of them tourists, Charley suspected, spilled from the pavements into the narrow streets. Car horns sounded, impatient Italian drivers gesturing from open windows, and a crocodile of uniformed school-children caught her eye as the crowds and the

traffic spilled out into another square domi-
nated by an ancient church. To their left was the
river, but Raphael turned right.

'This is the Via de' Tornabuoni,' he told
Charley. 'At the next intersection you will see
the Palazzo Strozzi, belonging to the family
who once plotted against the Medicis and paid
for their crime with banishment.'

The street was lined with imposing buildings, many of them housing designer shops,
and the pavement was busy with elegantly
clothed women who held themselves with that
confidence that Charley thought uniquely con-
tinental. Charley was so busy watching one of
them stepping out of a store that it took her by
surprise when Raphael suddenly turned into a
narrow opening between the buildings,
guarded by a pair of heavily studded wooden
doors. The doors opened automatically, allowing Raphael to drive in, then down a ramp into
an underground car park.

'This building was rebuilt in the eighteenth
century and originally came into the family via

marriage,' he explained to Charley once they were out of the car and standing in a lift. 'It fell into disrepair after my parents' death. I had it restored, but decided to retain only two of its five floors and let out the others.'

The lift had stopped, allowing them to step out of it and into a magnificent eighteenth-century marble hallway, with curved niches containing polished marble busts, and a wrought-iron banister curling upwards with the marble staircase. But where Charley imagined gilt-framed traditional family portraits must have once hung on the staircase wall, the walls now had a distinctly modern air to them, with their dark grey paint and their white-framed black and white photographs of street scenes and buildings. The effect somehow suited the hallway. It certainly spoke of a man who had the confidence and the arrogance to follow his own artistic instincts rather than adopt those of someone else. She couldn't imagine herself having the confidence to impose such a modern style on a traditional building.

'I don't employ any staff here; I use a con-
cierge service instead,' Raphael was informing
her. 'I will show you to your room, so that you
can leave your things there, and once you have
done that I suggest you rejoin me in the living
room, which is through that door to the left of
us.'

She and Raphael were going to be alone in
the apartment? Charley fought to remain
composed as she followed Raphael towards
the stairs, wide enough for them to climb side
by side, thankfully with a good few inches
between them.

The room Raphael showed her to was furnished in a French empire style and decorated
in soft blue, grey and white. It had, as she discovered once Raphael had left her to 'make
herself at home', a huge *en suite* bathroom,
with an enormous claw-footed bath and
several wall mirrors gilded with swags and
cherubs. Charley could easily imagine
someone like Napoleon's sister Pauline
relaxing in the deep tub as she gloated over her

brother's conquest of Italy. Despite its delicate colour scheme, somehow the rooms possessed an air of sensuality that reminded Charley of her own awkwardness. This was a bedroom for a woman confident in her sexuality—a purring, sensual seductress of a woman, who wore silks and satins and spent long, lazy summer afternoons lying in the arms of her lover.

Was this where Raphael brought his lovers? Sophisticated, knowing women who— Quickly Charley clamped down on thoughts she had no right to have, and which were an intrusion on Raphael's privacy that surely shamed her just as much as the betraying ache which had now started to pulse through her lower body. She must not let herself feel like this. She must not and she would not, Charley assured herself as she made her way back downstairs—just in time to see a small plump man stepping out of the lift to shake Raphael's hand.

'Charlotte, your timing is excellent,' Raphael told her. 'Come and meet my friend, Paulo

Franchetti. It is Paulo who has acted as go-between for us with Niccolo Volpari.'

Impossible for her to pull away when Raphael reached out to take hold of her arm and draw her towards them.

'*Buongiorno*, Charlotte.' Paulo greeted her with a smile and a handshake.

Fifteen minutes later, after a brief discussion about the garden, Paulo left. Flicking back the cuff of his pale blue shirt, Raphael studied his watch and then told her, 'Soon we shall have some lunch, but first there is something else we have to do.'

Since he was already striding towards the main door to the hallway, plainly expecting her to follow him, there was nothing else Charley could do.

The moment he opened the door bright sunlight streamed in, making Charley blink.

'This way,' Raphael directed her, putting his hand beneath her elbow and taking the outside edge of the pavement. Somehow, almost miraculously, the crowd seemed to part to allow them through, and within a few short yards Raphael came to a halt in front of the plate glass windows of the store of an internationally famous Italian designer of women's clothes.

'You will need a working wardrobe commensurate with your position,' Raphael informed her. 'We may as well deal with that now, whilst we are here in Florence.'

Charley looked at him.

'I have plenty of clothes at home that my sisters can send out to me.'

Raphael raised one eyebrow in a way that made her face burn.

'Let me guess: these clothes that you have at home are dull, plain garments that are two sizes too big for you? *Si?* They will not be suitable for your new role. You will be dealing with artists and craftsmen who value beauty— Italian men,' he emphasised. 'It is vitally important, since you are representing me, that they respect you and recognise that you understand the importance of quality craftsmanship.

To the master stonemason the correct drape of fabric against a woman's body is as important to his artistic eye as the correct choosing of a piece of stone, and that applies to all those with whom you will be dealing. In addition to that there will be many occasions on which I shall require you to accompany me to meetings and business dinners. Tonight, for instance, I do not want…'

'Me to show you up with my dull plain clothes?' Charley finished for him. 'Well, in that case I'm surprised you've brought *me* here instead of…of some elegant clotheshorse.'

'Why does the thought of wearing beautiful clothes fill you with such panic? Most women…'

'I am not most women, and it does not fill me with panic,' Charley denied. But of course he was right. She couldn't tell him, though, that she was afraid of beautiful clothes because she knew they would only underline how unworthy she was of wearing them.

'What I was actually going to say,' Raphael

continued, 'was that most women would wish to be dressed appropriately in the company of other women—particularly Italian women, who take a pride in their appearance. You will feel uncomfortable if you are not comparably clothed.'

No, she wouldn't, Charley wanted to say, because she knew how unsuited she was to the kind of Italian elegance to which Raphael was referring.

'You have already agreed to work under my direction and to abide by my conditions,' Raphael reminded her.

'As project manager, not in telling me what to wear,' Charley retorted. 'Work clothes for me mean a sturdy pair of boots and a properly fitting hard hat.' Was that really pity she could see in Raphael's gaze?

'You shall have those, of course, but I hardly think that even you would want to dress in such things for dinner.'

His words were a statement and not a question, Charley recognised, and, much as she would have liked to argue the point, Raphael was turning away from her, nodding to the uniformed doorman to open the door to the store, signalling that any attempt at rebellion on her part simply would not be tolerated.

Now Raphael's hand under her elbow felt like a form of imprisonment, but despite everything she believed about herself, humiliatingly, Charley was forced to admit that, when the sultry-looking sales assistant who had glided forward cast an assessing glance over her, she was glad she was wearing good-quality clothes—even though at the same time she felt acutely conscious of how badly her looks and lack of self-confidence at being in this most feminine of female places compared to that of the sales assistant. Not that the sales assistant spent much time in looking at her—she was far too busy looking at Raphael for that, Charley thought acidly. But then an older woman came forward, dismissing the other girl, smiling warmly but professionally at Raphael.

'My assistant is in need of a new wardrobe,' Raphael told the saleswoman. 'She will need everyday clothes, at least two business suits, and cocktail and evening dresses.'

No, Charley wanted to protest, not dresses. She never wore dresses. Her mother had always said that she was too much of a tomboy to wear them, and had laughed at her on the rare occasions when Charley had insisted that she wanted to be dressed like her sisters, telling her, 'Oh, poppet, you can't wear that.' Dresses—indeed all feminine clothes—were Charley's enemy. Just looking at them in shop windows brought her out in a cold sweat of remembered childhood humiliation.

The sales assistant's dark gaze, sent once in Charley's direction, didn't return to her as she nodded her head.

'Please come this way,' she invited them.

Within two minutes they were inside a private trying-on suite, complete with newspapers, magazines and a television, coffee having been ordered for them both.

Charley was then whisked into a luxuriously equipped large changing room, where she was measured by the saleswoman and then allowed to return to the main room of the suite, where Raphael was drinking his coffee whilst studying his BlackBerry.

Two young assistants were summoned and given a volley of instructions in Italian so rapid that Charley couldn't keep up with it, though she strained to catch the dreaded word 'dress' so that she could counteract it.

Swiftly, under the saleswoman's silent eagle-eyed inspection, the clothes rail which had been brought into the room was filled with clothes— beautiful, elegant clothes, in wonderful fabrics and sophisticated colours. Two trouser suits, both black; smartly tailored shorts in black, tan and white; tee shirts and knits; blouses… Charley's panic and dread were increasing with each new item added to the rail.

It was, of course, the evening dress that did it in the end: a swathe of cream silk satin, studded here and there with tiny crystals, the fabric so delicate that it fluttered sensually in the movement from the air-conditioning. Even without having seen it properly Charley knew instinctively that it was a gown designed for a woman who was confident of her own attractiveness—a woman who knew that when people looked at her the looks would be looks of admiration. She could just imagine the humiliation she would suffer if she allowed herself to be forced into such a dress; she would look idiotic, make a laughing stock of herself, the beauty and elegance of the dress simply underlining her own lack of them. The silk dress shimmered in front of her, warning her of the humiliation that was to come—inside her head she could hear her mother's voice, as she stood with Charley and her sisters in the children's department of Manchester's poshest store—Kendals on Deansgate—where she'd taken them to buy Christmas party dresses. She had been seven, Charley remembered.

She could see herself now, reaching out longingly towards a deep sea-green shot taffeta dress with a black velvet bodice and a wide sash, and then her mother had exclaimed, 'Oh, no, Charley—you couldn't possibly wear that.'

Just remembering the incident now, Charley could feel the sting of humiliation burning up under her skin, brought on by her mother's words and her own awareness of people turning to look at her, no doubt contrasting her with her pretty sisters.

Unable to stop herself, she stood up.

'I can't possibly wear any of these clothes,' she told Raphael agitatedly, too wrought up to notice the discreet manner in which the saleswoman had whisked her assistants and then herself out of the room.

'Why not?' Raphael was in no mood for female histrionics. He'd been awake in the early hours, questioning himself as to the wisdom of spending the night alone in his apartment here in Florence with Charley, and not very much liking the answers he had been forced to come up with.

And now, when he had decided that he had no alternative other than to make the best of the situation and see to it that she was properly prepared in every way to do the job for which he had hired her, the last thing he wanted was Charlotte behaving like a drama queen over him providing her with the clothes she so obviously needed.

'*Why not*? Isn't it perfectly obvious?' Charlotte demanded bitterly. 'Just look at them, and then look at me. There's no way I'm going to try them on when I know I can't wear those kind of clothes. I'll look ridiculous and…make a fool of myself.'

Catching a note in her voice that was close to hysteria, Raphael put down the paper he had been reading and stood up, his irritation forgotten.

Charley was shaking, close to tears, and there was a look of deep self-loathing and misery in her eyes. The fact that her self-control was so obviously close to breaking was enough to arouse instincts within Raphael that he couldn't ignore or deny. How could he call himself a man and ignore her distress? His parents had brought him up to be chivalrous and protective of the female sex, and besides… But, dangerously, her distress was also awakening other instincts within him— the instincts of a man who desired a woman. Of the two of them, only he knew how close he was to taking her in his arms and holding her there— and only he must know, Raphael warned himself, because once he had taken her in his arms there would be no going back. His pulse and then his body quickened, confirming what he already knew.

'Why on earth should you think that?' he demanded, and the curtness his own conflicted feelings had injected into his voice increased Charley's misery.

There was a long pause whilst Charley looked away from him, and then, as though the words were being wrenched from her, she replied to him.

'Because I do—that's all.'

It was a child's reply, defiance—a defence

against something too painful to reveal. Raphael knew that because he knew exactly how it felt not to be able to admit the true cause of an inner pain that had gone too deep for comfort.

Why had she said what she had? Why had she let him see her vulnerability? Why had she given him the weapon with which he could destroy her? It was too late now to ask herself those questions, Charley knew.

'I see.' Raphael paused. Charley trembled inwardly in the long pause whilst Raphael assessed the situation. What had he wanted most as a child, when confronted by his own pain and fear? Hadn't it been reassurance that there was in reality nothing to fear? A statement made confidently by 'a higher authority'? He had not received that reassurance because it had been impossible for his mother to deny the inheritance that was his, and even all her love had not been enough to protect him from that harsh reality. A woman's confidence in herself as a woman was everything. He had seen that in his mother, and somehow he wanted very much to restore it to Charley. But between that thought and acting upon it lay a no-man's land, and Raphael knew that he would be crossing a dangerous line within himself if he crossed that space.

He could stop. He could turn away from her. He could…

'Well, the choice is yours, but personally my judgement is that this dress would suit you very well indeed. You have the figure for it, and you carry yourself well, with elegance— something that not all women do.'

Too late now. He had crossed it. And in doing so had set in motion the situation he had sworn to himself he would avoid.

Charley could only stare at Raphael, her lips parting and then closing again. Raphael had complimented her. Raphael had said she carried herself well—with elegance. Raphael believed she could wear the dress.

A feeling—dizzying, euphoric, boundless in all that it offered her—flooded through her like a dam breaking, washing clean everything that lay before it, carrying away in its flood the detritus of all that was rank, festering and poisoned, leaving her feeling so different, so lightened, that she looked down at herself in a bemused fashion, as though her body was unfamiliar to her and something she had to learn to know and understand. 'Elegance?' she repeated wonderingly.

Raphael nodded his head, and told her, 'Try on the clothes and see for yourself.'

There was no time for any further private conversation. The saleswoman had returned, accompanied by a girl carrying a fresh tray of coffee—a discreet excuse for having left them, to save *her* face, Charley recognised, as she allowed herself to be ushered back into the changing room.

Once there, Charley quickly discovered that there was far more to buying new clothes Italian-style than she had ever imagined. For a start, there was the make-up, applied deftly and determinedly by another impossibly pretty, slender girl dressed, as they all were, in black. Only when she was satisfied was Charley allowed to step into the first of the two black trouser suits and a cream silk shirt. All the time Charley was forbidden to look at her own reflection until everything was done. Was it for her benefit or Raphael's that her hair was brushed and tamed? Or was it more likely because of the size of the potential sale that she was getting all this attention? Charley couldn't help wondering, a little cynically. It didn't matter what the reason was in the long run because the result would be the same: she would look like a garish caricature; she already knew that.

Only when she was finally allowed to look in the mirror she didn't look like a caricature at all. Instead she looked… As she stared at her reflection, Charley blinked her mascaraed lashes uncertainly. Her lashes looked so long, and her eyes looked so…so big, their colour somehow deeper thanks to the subtle addition of expertly placed eyeshadow, she recognised distractedly. She was putting off the moment when she would have to look again at her whole reflection, just in case she had been wrong and the miracle that seemed to have taken place had been more of a mirage than a miracle.

Guardedly and carefully, fearfully almost, Charley let her focus move downwards, past her mouth with its soft sheen of warm pink lipstick, down to where the open neck of the silk shirt revealed the little hollow at the base of her neck in a way that made her want to touch the unfamiliar vulnerability it revealed. Still she was holding back from fully looking at herself. But the saleswoman was walking towards the door, and Charley knew that soon she would have to show herself to Raphael. She looked quickly into the mirror, holding her breath, and the air leaked from her lungs as she met the image looking back at her, and saw that the miracle had actually happened.

That *was* her—that immaculately groomed, slender-looking, feminine young woman with long legs and fragile wrist bones. What magic was this? How could a simple trouser suit bring about such a transformation? Or was she after all just imagining it? Seeing in herself what she so desperately wanted to see? Believing what Raphael had told her because she wanted to believe it? Torn between hope and doubt, Charley blinked away threatening tears. There was only one way to find out. It was said that the eyes could not lie—perhaps only when she stood in front of him would she really know what Raphael truly thought.

When she walked into the room he put down his paper and looked at her, but it was impossible for Charley to tell what he was thinking from his expression. Something—a small swell of chagrin and disappointment—formed inside her.

She turned on her heel—or rather on the heels she had been given to wear to try on the suit—totally unaware of the instinctive and wholly female affronted flounce in the movement of her body.

Raphael saw it, though.

'So are we agreed that I was right?' he said dryly.

Charley knew that he was, but she wasn't prepared to give in.

'My parents—' she began defensively, only to be stopped when Raphael spoke again.

'Whatever your parents or anyone else might have said, whatever they might have believed, ends now and is in the past. Only the weak blame their past for the faults they find in their present; the strong acknowledge the effects of their past and then move on from it. We are all free to choose whether we will be weak or strong.' His gaze challenged her to make her choice.

Charley took a deep breath. She felt dizzy again, light-headed, sort of untethered—as though something within her was floating free. As she struggled to understand what she was feeling she heard Raphael addressing the hovering saleswoman.

'We will take everything.'

'But I haven't tried everything on yet,' Charley tried to protest.

'There's no need. I am sure they will all fit perfectly—and besides, it's nearly two o'clock and as yet we haven't had any lunch.'

Charley could see that there was no point in trying to argue or protest.

By the time she had changed back into her own clothes everything was arranged. Her new things would be packed up and delivered to the apartment, and would be waiting for her when she returned there.

They had lunch in a small restaurant down an alleyway that opened out into a courtyard basking in sunshine, with tubs of spring flowers in bright bloom, but despite the relaxed ambience of the setting it wasn't a pleasant lunch. Raphael barely spoke to her, responding to her attempts to make conversation by asking him about the city with such terse replies that Charley lost her appetite, along with the desire to continue trying to converse with him. He was obviously bored with her company, and her heart turned over inside her chest and went leaden with pain when she saw him looking in the direction of a stunning redhead who was walking past their table. No doubt he was wishing that he was with the redhead instead of her, Charley guessed miserably.

She tried not to let her feelings show as he flicked back his cuff and glanced at his watch, as though impatient for their lunch to be over. She'd been a fool to hope as they left the shop that he might offer to show her something of the city.

It had been a mistake to bring Charlotte here to this small restaurant for lunch, Raphael recognised, irritated with himself for the way his desire for her was weakening him. The intimacy of the restaurant made him ache for the even greater intimacy of his bedroom, and Charlotte naked in his arms on the bed within it. There was no logical reason why she should have this effect on him. He had, after all, known and resisted far more openly sexual women. But the sunlight striking through the windows warmed the pale skin of her throat, making him want to touch it, to possess the tiny pulse he could see beating at its base, to possess *her*. This was madness. He couldn't allow himself to be controlled by his desire for her. It would be breaking all the rules he had made for himself.

'I have some meetings this afternoon.'

At last Raphael was speaking to her, even if his voice was abrupt and cold. Charley focused on him as he summoned the waiter and asked for the bill. Was it because of this morning and the clothes? Was he already regretting allowing her to work on the project? She made herself think about how she would feel if he were to change his mind. The surge of emotion within told her immediately. She wanted desperately to work on the garden project, she realised. She wanted to prove herself—wanted to be herself.

The same sense of shock and recognition she had felt staring at her new reflection in the mirror of the changing room hit her again now, bringing with it an awareness that deep down inside herself she had longed for the opportunity to overturn the conceptions about herself that imprisoned her; had secretly yearned not to be clumsy, awkward Charley, but someone else instead. Before she had told herself that that was impossible, that she was what she was. Now, though, she was suddenly able to see that Raphael had been right when he had said that what she had been was what others had forced on her. The prospect of shedding that persona and its restrictions might be uncomfortable and alarming, but it was also exciting, Charley recognised, and was filled with new possibilities, new goals, new ambitions—just as she had been filled with a sense of mingled anxiety and delight when she had come face to face with her new image in the mirror. She was filled with those same feelings at the knowledge of what she could be if only she had the courage to seize the opportunity life and Raphael had given her.

She had always longed to visit this part of Italy and now she was here; she had always ached and yearned for a job that would allow her to express herself artistically, and now she had one. She wanted desperately to learn more and grow as a person now she had that opportunity. Like tiny bolts of lightning her thoughts darted through her head, illuminating the darkest corners of her secret self. She could improve her Italian, explore the countryside, soak herself in Florence's artistic history, feel herself grow with the garden, do everything, *be* everything she had ever wanted to do and be. Except for wanting Raphael. That she could not and must not do. That was a closed door and must remain so. If with the birth of the new Charlotte that was happening within herself there was to come a desire to embrace her sexuality by taking a lover, then she must accept that that lover could not be Raphael.

The bill paid, Raphael told her, 'I suggest you spend the afternoon getting to know your way around the city, as that will be essential if you are to work efficiently. There will be occasions when you will have to come here alone—which reminds me that you will need a car.'

'Only something inexpensive…' Charley put in. She had cost him so much already, but she was determined that the work she would do for the garden would more than repay that expenditure.

'And small, please,' she added, remembering the narrowness of the streets.

A waiter was hovering, ready to pull out her chair for her, and Raphael stood up, signalling that it was time for them to leave.

As they walked out into the sunshine of the courtyard Charley warned herself that she would need to buy herself some decent sunglasses to replace the cheap pair she had brought from home. Raphael was already reaching for his—classically shaped, with a discreet Cartier logo—and their dark glass completely obscured his eyes. If he had already looked male and dangerous, the sunglasses brought a sharper raw edge to that look, making her heart turn over and her senses thrill with female sensual speculation and expectation. Coupled with a desire to make him equally aware of her it brought a new strand to everything else that she was discovering about herself. It was just as well, she decided, that Raphael quite plainly did not find her attractive—otherwise this new desire to explore and adventure could take her very quickly out of her depth, because if Raphael were to indicate that he wanted her, then…

Then what? Charley asked herself as they parted outside the restaurant and she turned to make her way to the square, following one of the many helpful signs. Then she would fling herself into a brief sexual affair with him with hedonistic abandon, relishing the opportunity to give in to what she had already been feeling? Her heart thudded—not with apprehension and shock, but with excitement and anticipation.

Deep in her own thoughts, she didn't see the

good-looking young man coming the other way until she had bumped into him. Flushed and guilty, she began to apologise, but instead of merely walking on the young man removed his sunglasses to smile at her, revealing white teeth. His voice was as liquid with warmth as the look in his eyes as he told her, simply and approvingly, *'Si bella, signorina,'* and then swept her with a look of meltingly delicious male approval before moving on.

He had been little more than a boy, really, probably still in his late teens, his early twenties at the most, with a mop of dark curls and that male lankiness that young men possessed, but his compliment had still boosted her confidence, Charley admitted as she continued to walk down the street.

Watching her from the pavement a few yards from the restaurant, Raphael frowned and then turned on his heel. What did it matter to *him* if other men found Charlotte Wareham attractive?

CHAPTER EIGHT

SHE had had a wonderful afternoon, Charley reflected as she sat in a small café, drinking her cappuccino. One glance at the queues of people waiting to visit some of Florence's most famous sites had told her that with only an afternoon at her disposal her time would be put to its best use if she simply wandered around and got a feel for the city—which was exactly what she had done. She had walked down from the Via de Tornabuoni to the River Arno, and then along its embankment until she reached the Ponte Vecchio, wandering by the long queues for the Uffizi to gaze in delight at everything in the Piazza della Signoria. Picking up a free map from a tourist office, she had strolled at her leisure, pausing frequently to admire her surroundings and to drink in the wonderful atmosphere of the city. Inside her head she had removed its modern-day crowds and re-peopled its streets with men and women of the Renaissance, imagining them going about their everyday business.

Now, though, it was nearly four o'clock, and she still had an hour to spare before she had to return to the apartment. A girl walking past, dark hair swinging on her shoulders like liquid silk, caught her attention. Italian women had such lovely hair… She reached up and touched her own. She'd tied it back again during the afternoon, but the new Charlotte who was emerging from the old Charley wasn't satisfied any longer with the plain practicality of simply pushing her hair out of the way. She wanted a hairstyle that matched her new self. She'd passed any number of hair salons on her stroll—but how to find the right one? She could see the store where Raphael had taken her down the street to her left. Determinedly, before her courage could desert her, Charley finished her cappuccino and, having paid for it, made her way towards it.

If the saleswoman who had served them earlier was surprised by her request she gave no sign of it, listening calmly instead, and immediately announcing that she knew the very place and that if Charley would kindly wait for a second she would telephone them herself, on Charley's behalf.

Which was how, nearly two hours later, Charley found herself stepping out of the salon with an elegant, sleek, not quite shoulder-length newly bobbed hairstyle, which she liked so much that she couldn't help sneaking glances at herself in shop windows, unable to resist moving her head just for the pleasure of feeling her hair swing so perfectly against her neck.

But she wasn't going to have much time in which to get changed for dinner. The new haircut had taken far longer than she had expected…

* * *

Raphael looked at his watch. Charlotte should have been back over an hour ago, and her failure to return—initially an irritation—had now grown into an anxiety that was manifesting itself within him as anger that he was fighting to control.

Anger. Just thinking about the dangers of allowing himself to feel such an emotion intensified what he was trying *not* to feel. Was this a manifestation of the madness that ran in his blood? A feeling of irritation that would ultimately grow into a monstrous, many-headed alien form within him that he could not control? That would make him lash out, at first verbally, then physically, hurting and then destroying those who aroused the rage that had taken possession of him? That rage had already possessed him once, and he had sworn that he would never allow it to do so again.

The buzz of the apartment's intercom, followed by the sound of Charley's voice, cut across his thoughts, replacing them with action as he moved quickly towards the door of his study-cum-office.

Standing on the step outside the imposing double doors in the still busy street, not hearing any response to her call, Charlotte was just about to try the intercom again when the door suddenly opened to reveal Raphael standing there.

'You were supposed to return here at five-thirty. It is now nearly seven o'clock.'

He was angry, Charley recognised. 'I know—I'm sorry,' she apologised. 'I got stuck in the hairdressers. I didn't realise it would take so long, and I couldn't let you know as I don't have your mobile number.'

She'd been in a *hairdressers*? Raphael looked at the shining, elegant swing of her hair as she stepped out of the door's shadow, and was filled with an irrational surge of fresh anger as he recognised how much confidence and pleasure her new hairstyle was giving her, and that his concern for her wellbeing had been totally unnecessary.

'In future it would be as well if you remember that I don't pay you to visit hairdressers,' he told her harshly, adding, 'We have a vitally important business meeting in less than an hour's time, prior to which I had intended to run through a few things with you.'

Charley was completely mortified, all her pleasure in her new hairstyle lost, destroyed by the force of Raphael's anger.

'I'm sorry. I didn't think it would take so long. I wanted...' Her throat locked protectively around the words that would have humiliated her even more had she uttered them—told him that she had wanted him to look at her and admire her. Admire her or desire her? The confidence and happiness she had felt earlier had gone.

'I'll go and get changed,' she told Raphael in a flat voice that echoed what she was feeling.

Raphael watched her go, resisting the temptation to stop her and tell her—tell her what? That he wanted her? Wanted her when he knew that ultimately he might destroy her, and with her himself? The sooner everything was sorted out and he was able to leave her in charge of the garden project the better. He had work to do in Rome with regard to his business interests, which would keep him safely away from her for long enough for him to deal with his unwanted desire for her, Raphael assured himself.

In her bedroom, Charley undressed and then showered quickly, glad that the stylist had taken the time to show her how to dry and smooth her hair to keep it in polished perfection. She had taken the opportunity to ask the saleswoman at the designer store which of Charlotte's new outfits she would recommend for a smart business dinner engagement, and so, wrapped in a towel, she removed the clothes the saleswoman had suggested from the wardrobe in the dressing room off her bedroom and carried them carefully to place them on the bed.

The outfit was a slim-fitting sleeveless cream dress, over which went a soft, floating, seamed and tucked tunic top, with long sleeves that flared out at the wrist to almost cover her hands. The tunic reached almost to the hem of the dress, and the outfit was completed by a fine-knit silk jersey double-breasted cardigan jacket, cropped just above the waist.

A little dubiously Charlotte put each piece on, and then went and looked uncertainly in the mirror, exhaling a sigh of shaky delight when she saw that, far from looking as though she was dressed in an odd assortment of clothing, the finished effect was a breathtakingly delicate yet sophisticated blending of textures and fabrics.

Boosted by the new confidence, Charley slipped on the strappy wedge sandals that complemented the outfit, and picked up the pretty soft leather clutch bag that went with them. It was just about large enough to hold a notepad and pen, as well as her lipstick and comb. She headed for the door, stepping out onto the landing just as Raphael emerged from his own room.

Charley held her breath a little, wondering if

he would make any comment about her appearance, and then told herself when he didn't
that she wasn't really disappointed. He was
wearing a light-coloured suit over a dark
shirt—the effect, to her mind's eye, very
Italian and very sexy.

As he waited for her at the top of the stairs
he reached into his pocket and produced a
small oblong package, which he handed to
her, telling her, when she looked uncertainly
at him, 'Scent. Later on you can choose your
own, but for now this will have to do. No
Italian woman considers herself properly
dressed without her favourite perfume, and
I'm aware that you don't wear any.'

Aware too, Raphael acknowledged inwardly,
that the scent she always carried with her that
was simply her own was becoming dangerously embedded in his senses. He had been
glad of the shadows on the landing when she
had come out of her room; he might have seen
the clothes the saleswoman had chosen
hanging on their rail, but the effect of the

blending of different fabrics and textures of the outfit she was now wearing, and the way they both concealed and yet at the same time subtly hinted at the curves of her body, was one of sensual promise. And he would not be the only man to think that, Raphael knew. The feeling that speared through him was viciously sharp. *Jealousy?* He did not *want* other men to look at her with desire? He had no right to feel like that, Raphael told himself grimly.

Scent! She had not thought of buying any herself. Charley's fingers trembled as she removed the wrapping, just as they would have done if this had been a lover's gift—which of course it was not.

The liquid in the small glass bottle was the colour of warm amber. Very carefully Charley removed the top, breathed in the scent, and immediately fell in love. It transported her to summer gardens filled with fat, blooming heavy-petalled roses, their sweetness spiced with something alluringly exotic that made her think of Eastern harems and velvet nights.

She'd expected Raphael to choose her something modern and practical, but this surely was a scent designed for a woman who luxuriated in her sensuality—a scent she would wear in bed at night to clothe her naked body in temptation for her lover.

'If you don't like it—' Raphael began.

'I do,' Charley assured him, determinedly dabbing it on her throat and wrists in proof of her claim. 'It's heavenly—but there's no label on it.'

'It's from a *parfumier* who blends his own scents.' His manner was off-hand and dismissive, making Charley feel reluctant to pursue the subject, although she loved the scent so much she desperately wanted to know where it had come from. She already knew that when the bottle was empty she would want to replace it.

Charley had only just dabbed the scent on her wrists and throat, but already Raphael could smell its sensual mix of promise and passion and Charley herself. He had had to smell several different scents before he had found the one he had eventually chosen. Even though he had been aware of its sensuality, he hadn't, he admitted to himself now, been prepared for the effect it would have when mixed with the warmth of Charley's skin. His mother had always worn a rose-based scent, less sensual and more floral. He pushed away that memory. He didn't know why Charley's presence was making him think so often of his mother, and nor did he want to know.

CHAPTER NINE

IT MIGHT be over now, but Charley had had the most wonderful evening ever. The conversation had been every bit as intoxicating for her as the wine that had filled her glass. To be amongst people who were so knowledgeable about their craft, so filled with passion for all that it repre-sented, and who treated her as their equal, had made her feel so complete and comfortable with herself that every minute of the evening had been a joy. The whole evening had been the most ex-hilarating and wonderful experience. Antonio and Niccolo were both in their early fifties, and their wives, Charley guessed, in their late forties, mothers of grown-up families. They had treated Charley with kindness, complimenting her on her appearance and asking her about her own family circumstances, issuing invitations for her to join their own family get-togethers whilst she was working in Italy, so that she would not feel alone. And Niccolo had assured Raphael that he was interested in the project, and would be willing to have his teachers and students involved in it. A coup in which Charley hoped she had played her part.

Now, though, they were back at the apartment, and Raphael hadn't said a word to her—his silence on the drive back a continuation of his behaviour towards her during the evening. Because he had been watching her? Assessing her? Testing her to see if she was up to the job of managing his project?

With her new-found confidence, instead of giving in to her anxiety she met it head-on.

'Something seems to be wrong. If it's because of the garden and my job, and you've changed your mind…'

She was not allowed to get any further. Raphael swung round and told her harshly, 'It isn't because of the garden, or your job. It's because of *this*.'

If he'd been fighting his desire for her only this evening he would have been able to control it. But he hadn't. He'd been fighting it for day after aching day, night after sleepless night, minute by minute, second by second, until the sheer weight of what he was trying to hold back was such that all it had taken was that one small extra burden of her question to tear down the walls he had built against her effect on him. In the few seconds of time it took him to reach for her a whole world of sensual images and longings flashed through him—an unstoppable avalanche of self-destruction he was powerless to stop.

Charley could hardly believe it. She was where she had so longed to be: in Raphael's arms, in his hold, his mouth hard on hers, her senses bursting into life. For a brief handful of seconds she was sharply aware of the soft darkness of the hallway, the smell of Raphael's cool cologne-scented skin contrasting with the heat they were generating, the rustle of their clothing, the soft sounds of pleasure she herself was making under Raphael's kiss and the sharp click of her heels touching the floor, because she'd raised herself up on tiptoe in order to get as close to him as she possibly could. And then she was aware of nothing other than the feel of Raphael's mouth on her own, the thrust of his tongue between her lips, and the surge of delight that invaded her body speared through her with a fierce urge to respond to him, to match him touch for touch and breath for breath.

This surely more than anything else was what she had been born for—what her senses had been designed for, what her inhibitions wanted to yield to. Curling her tongue against Raphael's in sensual pleasure, she pressed closer to him, feeling her breasts flatten against the hard muscular wall of his chest, knowing that her legs trembled as she leaned into him, knowing that inside herself she was softening and aching and wanting.

Her body's goal was Raphael's possession of it, and hedonistically, recklessly, perhaps even dangerously, she was welcoming every single sensation and thought that took her closer to that goal.

Lost in the heavy, pulsing need to give everything that she was, everything that she had, to the urgency driving through her, the sudden raw sound of Raphael's 'No!' as the harsh denial was ripped from his throat shocked her into frantic disbelief.

When Raphael released her and stepped back she swayed towards him, barely able to stand, her body shivering with rejection and the piercing, throbbing ache of denial, totally unable to comprehend why, having aroused her desire for him, he had now plunged her into such an aching agony.

'No? You can't say that. Not now—not after you've shown me that you want me and…and made me want you.'

She was so untutored in guile, so honest in what she thought and felt. Her words ripped into him, tearing apart the barrier he had tried to put between them.

'Want you?' Raphael laughed bitterly.

Until tonight, until he had seen her standing on the landing earlier, he had thought he had won, that he had subdued his desire for her—but all he had done was damp it down, and over the course of the evening, as he had watched her, it had leapt into fresh life like a wild fire, devouring everything that stood in its way.

'No, I do not want you,' he told her with brutal honesty. 'What I feel for you is no mere wanting. I wish to God that it were. I hunger for you. I ache for you and I crave you. But, since I have a rule of never mixing my business and my personal lives, those needs shall have to go unsatisfied. We will return to the *palazzo* in the morning, and then I shall leave for Rome.'

He was walking away from her, heading for the stairs. Charley licked her suddenly dry lips, and then, before she could change her mind, she ran after him, pushing past him on the stairs. She stood in front of him, spreading her arms so that he couldn't get past.

'Sometimes rules have to be broken,' she told him breathlessly. 'Sometimes things happen that we shouldn't try to control—things we are meant to experience, even if their pleasure is short lived.' She looked up at him. 'I want you to make love to me, Raphael. I want to know your hunger and your ache and your desire, because I feel them too.'

In the half-light of the hallway the shadows lent his face a haunted harshness, giving him the look of a man who belonged to another age, tormented and driven beyond his own limits.

'There can be no future for you with me,' he told her harshly.

'I am not asking you for a future.'

'Then what are you asking me for?'

'Tonight,' Charley told him softly. 'Tonight and nothing between us—nothing to stop us sharing the honesty of what we feel. When you said what you did earlier today, about my clothes and about my…my elegance, you started a process that has set me free to be myself. I want you to complete that process, Raphael.'

Charley could hear the increased pressure of his breathing even though he hadn't moved.

Holding his dark, unreadable gaze, she continued. 'I want you to take me and hold me. I want you to complete what you have begun, Raphael.'

His breathing had become a harsh sound of constraint, his chest openly rising and falling with the pressure he was exerting over himself.

Charley let her own voice drop and soften to a husky, sensual whisper.

'I want us to break your rules, Raphael. I want us to have what we can have together tonight.' She took a step towards him and waited, her heart pounding. Never in a thousand lifetimes had she imagined herself behaving like this with such sexual boldness, but now that she knew Raphael shared her desire she was prepared, whatever she had to risk, her whole body thrilling at the thought of what they could share.

When he reached out and circled her wrists with his hands, his fingers long and strong as steel when they snapped around her flesh, Charley's anticipation turned to dread. He was going to deny her—move her out of his way and step past her. His grip forced her arms down to her sides and held them pinioned there.

'One night?' he said softly. 'Do you really think that one night will be enough to sate the hunger you have aroused in me?' And then he was kissing her, fiercely and demandingly, and her own desire was leaping up inside her to meet the challenge of his.

CHAPTER TEN

THEY had reached the top of the stairs and they were still kissing, but Charley had no awareness of them having moved, no awareness of anything other than the heat of Raphael's mouth on her own and the need inside her that he was feeding.

Now, though, he had stopped kissing her. His hold of her wrists was slackening, his thumbs finding the excited race of her pulse and tormenting it with small circling caresses.

'There can be no future in this,' he warned her, as he had done before, emphasising the words as he spoke them.

'I don't want a future,' Charley told him, and believed it. 'I just want tonight and you.'

Raphael could feel the wild fire of unleashed passion surging through his body. It was too much. He couldn't deny her—or himself. The urge to hold her body against his own, skin to skin, roared through him, but somehow he held on to a final strand of self-control—for her sake as much as his own.

'Very well, but there is one condition I must make—one assurance I shall need from you.'

Charley waited. What was he going to say? That she must not fall in love with him? She knew *that* without him needing to tell her.

Raphael expelled the air from his lungs and breathed in slowly.

'There must be no risk of there being any consequences to our actions in the form of a child.'

Why did his words strike against her heart like a sledgehammer blow? She certainly hadn't been thinking of conception or children when she had so boldly begged him to break his rule.

'Naturally I shall take precautions myself to ensure…'

'There's no need.' Charley stopped him. 'I'm

on the pill.' It was the truth, even if the reason she was taking it was because the anxiety of the last year had meant that she needed to take it to correct her monthly cycle.

'Very well, but I must warn you that should you conceive the pregnancy will have to be terminated.'

Shock jolted through her, icy cold, in instinctive rejection of what he was demanding.

But it wasn't his child she wanted, she reminded herself, it was Raphael himself. And she did want him—desperately.

He should stop this right now, Raphael urged himself. It wasn't too late. He could turn away—refuse what she was offering him. *Refuse?* When his body ached like hell for her, and his senses were already anticipating every single pleasure they would give one another? He was beyond stopping himself, beyond listening to any inner warning voices, beyond even questioning just why this woman of all women should have the power to overturn all the boundaries he had set in place.

Charley moved uncertainly, a sharp point of light from the heavy chandelier that hung from the ceiling throwing the soft curves of her breasts into relief. Her nipples were pushing against the fabric of her clothes, tight and erect, their message of sexual arousal making Raphael's own flesh harden. He released Charley's wrist and lifted his hand to her body, rubbing the pad of his thumb against the cresting flesh, feeling his own body react to the visible shudder that gripped Charley as she moaned softly in response to his caress. It was too late to turn back—too late to do anything other than give in to the need driving through him.

'This way.'

Raphael was taking her to *his* bedroom. A new quiver of sensation ripped through Charley. Somehow the thought of Raphael making love to her in his bed rather than her own added an extra layer of sensuality and delight to what she was already feeling.

* * *

Elegant and smart, like photographs she had seen of seriously expensive boutique hotel bedrooms, Raphael's bedroom was decorated in shades of off-white, dark grey and aubergine, with heavy silk curtains striped in those colours to match the linens on the large double bed.

Not that Charley was in the right frame of mind to appreciate the decor, nor indeed had the time, for no sooner had Raphael switched on the low-level lighting, and she had stepped inside, than he closed the door and took her back in his arms.

The touch of his hand on her breast, expertly finding the hard rise of her nipple, made her shudder with fresh delight, but Charley's conscience was beginning to intrude on her pleasure. Reluctantly she broke the kiss to admit to him, 'There's something I ought to tell you.'

'What?'

'Well…' Charley wrinkled her nose. 'The truth is that I haven't had much previous experience. I don't want to disappoint you…'

She could see his chest rise and then fall again. Had she put him off?

'Much or any?' Raphael questioned her.

He was too astute. She had known that before.

'Any,' she admitted, before asking him, 'Does that change things and put you off?'

'Do you want it to?'

'No!' Charley told him vehemently.

'The pleasure we shall give each other and share will be unique to us, exclusive to us, as it is with any lovers. But, like any man, I dare say my ego will enjoy knowing that I cannot be compared to a previous lover and found wanting.'

Charley was so relieved that she burst out truthfully, 'I can't imagine any woman ever thinking that about you.'

Raphael exhaled slowly, recognising that deep down inside himself he had already suspected he would be her first lover. His heart slammed into the wall of his chest. He wanted to take hold of her right now, slide the clothes from her body and give in to his desire to take them both to a place where all that mattered was their shared need for one another.

The realisation rolled over him that he wanted her as he had never wanted any other woman—as he had never imagined wanting any woman—but all he said to her was, 'I shall do my best to be worthy of your faith in me.' He was unable to stop himself from adding under his breath, 'I just hope that my self-control is up to the challenge.'

His self-control? Charley trembled under the eager anticipatory tightening of her body. She felt, she thought dizzily, as though sensually, sexually, her desire for him had bloomed into a peak of lush, ripe readiness. Almost magically she was free of all restraints and inhibitions, just as though she had been reborn into the full flowering of her own sexuality. Because of Raphael. And not just because she wanted him, but because he had shown her that she could be free of the damaging beliefs of her past, that she could be whatever she chose to be.

Her body was singing with excitement and joy, aching deliciously and oh, so tormentingly with a thousand aches that instinctively she knew would meld into one piercingly intense surge of need beneath Raphael's touch.

She looked up at him and smiled.

'It isn't your self-control that I want,' she told him simply.

Raphael felt the breath shudder through his lungs, the savage thrust of his desire crashing through his barriers.

'You shouldn't say such things to me,' he warned her as he closed the distance between them.

'Why not?' Charley whispered the words against his lips. She was trembling so violently that she had to hold on to him for support.

'Because it's dangerous, because *you* are dangerous—dangerously enticing, dangerously sensual, dangerously tempting me to forget all the reasons why I should not be doing this,' Raphael whispered back.

His hands were moving over her, angling her within his hold so that he could shape and knead the soft fullness of her breast as he kissed her. Pleasure rushed through her— pleasure, excitement, and a need that had her finding his tongue with her own and caressing it, twining with it. Wild shudders of firework explosive delight showered her when Raphael stopped her, to turn her explorative caress into the shockingly deep thrust of his tongue within the softness of her mouth, his tongue and his hand against her breast working to a rhythmic beat that produced an aching echo of its urgency deep inside her. Helplessly Charley pressed closer to him, her hands moving feverishly over his chest and then his shoulders, frustrated by the barrier of his shirt.

As though he knew how she felt, he moved his lips to her ear, demanding, 'What is it you want?'

'I want to touch you, all of you, without your clothes,' Charley answered him immediately, her voice unsteady with the intensity of her longing.

'Then take them off for me.'

Undress him? A shock wave of raw need

stormed through her, and then her fingers were tugging at his tie, trembling over his shirt buttons, only her longing to feel his bare skin against her own preventing her from being distracted by the way he was caressing her tight nipple whilst he held her shoulder with his free hand and slowly kissed his way along the side of her neck. At last she had his shirt unfastened, tugged out of the waistband of his suit trousers, and she was free to bury her face against the warm, muscular expanse of his chest with its soft covering of dark hair, breathing in the scent of him, pressing frantically hungry kisses on his bared skin, so completely lost in the pleasure of what she was at long last free to do that she was oblivious to the fact that Raphael had stopped kissing her and touching her, and was simply holding her whilst he struggled to control his breathing.

This was so much more than he had been prepared for—so much more than he had understood he could ever feel or want. Charley's open and uninhibited pleasure in what she was doing was undermining his self-control like the tide stealing away sand. Raphael cupped the sides of her head, arching his throat back in mute offering to the searing, scalding pleasure of her lips caressing his skin. An uncontrollable shudder of male pleasure seized him in its grip.

'Enough,' he told Charley rawly. 'Now it's my turn to undress you.'

Where she had been all fingers and thumbs, all out-of-control excitement and delight, Raphael was skilled. His touch was sure and knowing as he dealt with the layers of her clothes until she was standing in her under-wear—the delicate silk and lace lingerie that had been delivered with her new clothes.

In one of the mirrors set on either side of the bed above the bedside tables Charley could see the pale shimmer of her almost naked body, glowing and pearlescent in the subdued lighting of the room, the slenderness and delicacy of her bone structure made more fragile by the solid muscularity of Raphael's torso beside it.

'We look so different,' she told him, her voice husky, softened by desire.

'But together we will make a perfect whole,' Raphael answered her.

As she watched their reflections she saw Raphael's hand lift to her breast, to push down the silk fabric and expose the dark flesh of her nipple, hard and tight with arousal. The sight of it, knowing what its arousal meant, sent an urgent frisson of longing down her spine. As though Raphael had felt it and knew its meaning, he traced a line of fiery erotic kisses along her shoulderblade, whilst his fingertips plucked and teased the eager longing of her nipple, causing starburst after starburst of pleasure to spread through her. But that pleasure was nothing compared to the dark agony of desire that flooded her when Raphael took her nipple into his mouth, tonguing it; stroking it; making her arch her body up to him in helpless supplication, whilst her veins ran with liquid heat and her whole body pulsed to the rhythm of her longing.

His mouth still on her breast, Raphael slid his hands into the cut-away legs of her knickers, moulding and kneading the rounded cheeks of her bottom, making her press as close to him as she could as the ache between her legs intensified. She wanted him to touch her there. She wanted to press herself against him, to rub herself against him. She wanted— Charley gasped in shocked delight when Raphael lifted his head, his hand sliding between her legs, his fingers stroking the soft swell of flesh that covered her sex, pulling down the pretty confection of silk and lace so that in the mirror she could see the movement of his hand against her body, could see too that he was watching her just as she was watching him.

Slowly, so slowly that she had to hold her breath so as not to beg him to hurry, he parted the lips of her sex, causing a shudder of aroused delight to shake her body. Then she was arching with erotic shock when he stroked gently up and down the soft wet valley, and then pressed his fingers against the wellspring of her desire, rubbing it slowly, and then more swiftly, whilst she gasped and writhed and clung to him, her eyes wide with all that she was feeling. Her orgasm came so quickly and so intensely that it shook her from head to foot, and she needed the support of his arms to hold her as he kissed her and took the words of pleasure from her lips.

CHAPTER ELEVEN

STILL held in Raphael's arms, Charley could feel the hard, urgent pulse of his arousal against her as she relaxed into him, stirring a new surge of eager desire within her body that had her moving languorously against him; satisfied and yet at the same time aware of the capacity within her to be aroused to fresh need—aware too of a deep inner ache that had not been quenched.

What she had just experienced was the beginning, not the end, and the movement of her body against his was sending Raphael a deliberate message to that effect.

Even so he still hesitated, forcing down the impulse to carry her over to the bed and spread the softness of her body there beneath his own, so that he could enter her and lose himself in her in the way his flesh ached for him to do, but then Charley moved against him, pressing closer to him, snapping the tautly strung fragility of his self-control.

As though he had given his need words and spoken them to her, Charley whispered vehemently, 'Yes!' and within seconds he had removed the last of their clothes and they were on the bed, her body soft and eager beneath his hands.

This was wonderful, heaven, beyond anything she could ever have imagined. Raphael's skin felt like oiled silk beneath her explorative touch, his torso narrowing down to a flat belly, his body ridged with muscles beneath the warmth of his skin, and the reality of his erection a thousand times more breathtakingly erotic than any artistic phallic images she had ever seen. She reached out and stroked her fingertips along its length in wondering delight, gasping in sharp pleasure as her touch transferred the delicate stroke of Raphael's

tongue-tip against her earlobe to the hard possession of his mouth against her nipple, his
lips tugging on its pouting sensuality after its
earlier pleasuring. Instinctively she closed her
hand around him, her body shuddering as she
felt the fierce pulse beating from his flesh into
her own, and then arching on a spasm of sharp
pleasure when his teeth grated delicately
against the sensitive flesh of her nipple. Had
she thought that she now knew desire? She
had been wrong. What she had known had
been merely the foothills of a far greater
height.

Bending her head towards him, Charley
whispered to Raphael.

'I was right. You are the most wonderful
lover.'

'How can you know?' he mocked her softly,
kissing the valley between her breasts and then
making his way up towards her mouth.

'My body knows,' Charley answered him,
'and that is why it wants you so much.'

Ridiculous that a few words should have such

an intense effect on him, Raphael knew. But they had. It was time. He couldn't wait any longer.

Cradling Charley against his side with one arm, he reached towards the drawer in the bedside table with the other.

Guessing what he was seeking, Charley placed her hand on his chest and shook her head, telling him fiercely, 'No. I want to feel you inside me—just you. Your flesh against mine as nature intended. Not—not a…a chemical barrier that isn't you…I'm on the pill so we're safe. I want to feel you inside me, Raphael,' Charley repeated determinedly. 'Just you—all of you…' She was kissing him in between her words: eager, passionate little kisses that, like her touch on his body, showed him how much she wanted him.

He should ignore her pleas. He should behave sensibly. He should ignore the way his body had reacted when she had said she wanted him inside her. He should…

'I want you so much,' Charley whispered.

It was too much, and too late to stop himself

now, with the soft weight of her in his arms, her body lying eagerly open to his possession, her muscles closing tightly around him as he slowly thrust into her.

Charley shuddered and gasped, and then sighed with exalted pleasure, her hands gripping Raphael's shoulders as he moved slowly and carefully into her. Each sensation built on the pleasure of the one before it, as though she was climbing a set of steps. Her body protested, her muscles tightening to hold him where he was when Raphael pulled back a little, but his next thrust reassured her body that he wasn't leaving it, simply moving deeper and then deeper still, until she was moving with him, wrapping her legs around him, welcoming the increasing sensation of fullness and energy within her.

She was Eve and the apple—all the woman he could ever want, and impossible for him to resist. Her response to him was driving him both to want to conquer her and at the same time give all of himself over to her. His whole world had narrowed down to the bed and to her, one moment spread out beneath him, the next wrapped around him. The scent and sight of her, the sound of her pleasure, the feel of her skin under his hands, the hot, slick power of the way her body received and held him…

It was happening. It was coming. A flutter at first…but now the sensation gathered and gripped her. Charley sucked in a lungful of air and then tensed, her nails digging into the flesh of Raphael's shoulders as she looked up into his face.

His skin was sheened with sweat, the muscles in his arms corded and locked.

She held nothing back, Raphael recognised, concealed nothing. He could see the ecstasy in her expression as well as feel the surging rhythmic contractions of her orgasm. His own body trembled and then shook, his throat arching and his whole body pulled as taut as a bow in that final second before he joined her in his own release into pleasure.

CHAPTER TWELVE

CHARLEY looked up from the weekly progress chart she had been studying. It was three weeks now since Raphael had brought her back to the *palazzo* and left her there. She pushed back her chair from the pretty, delicately painted wood desk. She had been uncertain at first how Raphael would feel about the fact that Anna had given her as her office the pretty little sitting room which she had told her had last been used by Raphael's mother, but Anna had assured her that he wouldn't mind, that he had told her simply to make sure that Charley had somewhere to work.

Three weeks: twenty-one nights of unbearable aching longing, and twenty-one days of fighting to keep Raphael out of her thoughts.

She had had three wonderful days with him in Florence. Those she would never, ever forget. Three wonderful days and three even more wonderful nights: days during which Raphael had shown her his Florence, and nights when he had shown her the power of her own sexuality.

He might not have been a demonstrative lover in public, holding her hand and pulling her to him as she had seen one young man doing with his girl in the Boboli Gardens the afternoon Raphael had taken her there, but he had showed his desire for her in other more subtle ways— via a certain look, a certain touch—and there had definitely been no holding back from showing her his desire when they were on their own.

On their final morning before they had left the city she had been lying in his arms, after Raphael had made love to her. He had kissed her and smoothed the hair back off her face, telling her, 'You do understand, don't you, that what has happened here between us in Florence must belong only to Florence?'

Yes, she had understood—but that hadn't stopped her from asking him, almost begging him in desperation, even though she had already known what his answer would be, 'Will we come back?'

'No,' he had told her, with a finality that had cut into her like a knife slicing into her heart.

She had known, of course, that that would be his answer. He had told her from the start not to want anything more than they had had. Then she hadn't thought about the future— then she had been too driven by her desire for him to look deeper and see what was already growing beneath it. Then she hadn't realised that she had fallen in love with him. Not then, but she did now.

It wasn't Raphael's fault. It was her own. But knowing that didn't make her pain any easier to bear. She had tried to escape it by spending all her waking hours working. She was almost always the first at the garden in the morning and the last to leave at the end of the day, returning to the *palazzo* to write reports late into the evening, but not even that could keep Raphael out of her thoughts. He was there all the time, overshadowing everything else, and Charley knew that he always would be.

The nights were worse than the days. She'd delay going to bed until the early hours, convinced that she would be so exhausted that she would sleep, and she did. But only for a while, waking up often to find her pillow wet with her tears, her body and her heart aching for Raphael.

Charley looked round the pretty, feminine salon. Whenever she imagined Raphael's mother here, perhaps sitting at the desk where Charley herself worked, writing her letters, another image would appear: Raphael himself as a young boy. Her heart turned over inside her chest, a yearning spreading through her. Now she could understand, as she had never understood before, the need of a woman to conceive the child of the man she loved. To have that child as a living, breathing memorial of what they had shared, to be loved and cherished as a precious gift.

But of course there could be no such gift for her. Her all too brief span of time in the paradise that being Raphael's lover had created for her was over. Raphael himself had closed the gates on their return.

Wearily Charley looked down at the desk. It was far too small really, for the amount of paperwork she had to deal with, but Anna had offered her this room so proudly that Charley hadn't had the heart to tell the housekeeper that she needed a working space that was more functional.

So far they were ahead of schedule with the work of clearing the garden in readiness for the actual renovation—although Charley suspected that sometimes the contractors would have preferred it if she didn't put in such long hours, assessing the progress of everything. But working herself hard was the only way she had of trying to stop the pain of loving Raphael.

In a few minutes she would go downstairs and drive out to the site, and then this evening she would update her schedules for the week and input them into her computer, ready to send to Raphael with her report as she had done for the previous three weeks. So far, though, Raphael had not e-mailed her back— not even to say that he had received her reports. Because he was afraid that if he contacted her she would plead with him as she had done in Florence? It was Charley's prayer that she would *never* humiliate herself and irritate Raphael by doing that.

There were moments when she longed for the comforting presence of her sisters, so that she could unburden herself to them and be comforted by them, but then there were other times when she simply couldn't bear the thought of disclosing her pain and the reasons for it to anyone, because it was so raw.

'All the statues have now been removed. Those that are only slightly damaged will be repaired in my workshops in Florence, whilst those that cannot will be measured and photographed so that exact copies can be made.'

Charley nodded her head as she listened to Niccolo giving her his progress report. It had been a long day, and now the warmth was dying out of the sun as it sank towards the horizon.

'You'll let me have a detailed report to pass on to Raphael?'

'Of course. No work will be done until he has sanctioned it. As you know, we've already photographed each piece of statuary, and the location where it was found.'

Charley nodded her head again. She too had taken photographs of everything, meticulously numbering them and pinpointing the sites on her own personal plan of the garden. She wasn't going to take any chances of being found wanting in her professional capacity, even if Raphael had found her not good enough to keep in his bed.

'We are doing very well. Raphael will have every reason to be extremely pleased with our progress,' Niccolo told her, as he left to return to Florence.

Half an hour later Charley too was ready to call it a day. The last rays of the setting sun were fading as she locked the heavy gates. It would be dark by the time she returned to the *palazzo*, where she would shower and eat and then start work on her evening's paperwork.

Since it was Friday, once she had updated everything she could e-mail it to Raphael—her treat of the week, her only precious contact with him. Just thinking about e-mailing him made her stomach muscles cramp with a mixture of pain and longing—and the desperate hope that he would e-mail her back.

How pathetic she was, Charley derided herself contemptuously. She looked towards the small Fiat Raphael had given her to drive, and then looked again in disbelief when she saw the sleek sports car parked next to it.

'Raphael...' Without thinking, desperate to

get to him, she stepped into the road, oblivious to the car coming towards her until she heard the blare of its horn.

Raphael was out of the Ferrari in a flash, running faster than he had ever run in his life, grabbing hold of Charley and dragging her bodily out of the way as the car swerved to avoid her.

Charley felt the heat of its engine, the sting of the stones it threw up on her skin, and she heard the curses of the driver—but none of that mattered. All that mattered was that she was with Raphael. But he was shaking her, violently and almost painfully, over and over again, his face drained of colour, his hands hard on her arms as he demanded furiously, 'Why didn't you look before you crossed the road? Are you blind? What were you trying to do? Kill yourself?'

Charley had never seen him so angry. She could almost feel the heat and the power of his rage.

Shocked and frightened, more by her near-miss than by his anger, she trembled in his hold and begged him, 'Stop it.'

Immediately Raphael thrust her away from him, so hard that she staggered, and then leaned on the side of his car.

Reaction had begun to set in, reducing her to a shaking bundle of jelly-legged awareness of the danger she had been in.

'Get in,' Raphael ordered her, yanking open the door.

'I've got my own car,' Charley reminded him, but the last thing she felt like doing was driving.

'I'll arrange for that to be collected later.'

She was in the car, still feeling shaky and sick, wanting Raphael to hold her tenderly and comfortingly instead of being angry with her.

Raphael drove them back to the *palazzo* at speed, without speaking to her, and Charley was glad to be able to escape from him once they were inside, hurrying up to her room, wincing as she heard the furious slam of his office door on her way upstairs.

Ten minutes later, standing under the warm

sting of the shower, Charley began to feel slightly better. Her shock had receded, leaving her to admit that she had been careless, and that she was lucky that Raphael had acted so speedily to save her from going under the wheels of the car. That was what loving the wrong man did for you. It made you so desperate to be with him that you forgot everything else. She had to find a way to stop herself from loving him. She must.

Wrapping a towel round her wet body, she headed for the bedroom—and then came to an abrupt halt when she saw Raphael standing there, waiting for her.

He was still angry. She could see that immediately.

'I'm sorry—' she began, but he stopped her.

'Sorry? Is that all you can say?' he demanded harshly. 'You damn nearly kill yourself and…' He was reaching for her again, but Charley stepped back from him.

'No!' she uttered, panicking, not trusting herself to let him touch her, knowing that if he did she would end up begging him to stay with her.

Her denial was too much for Raphael. His heart was still thudding with the agony he had felt when he had thought the car would hit her. Everything he had told himself and taught himself was forgotten. He was a man denied what was rightfully his, the woman who was rightfully his—the woman fate had devised for him and bequeathed to him, the woman whose only previous 'no' to him had been a plea for him not to leave her.

Charley could almost feel Raphael's tension. It showed in his abrupt movements and in the dark grimness of his eyes, as though he was only just managing to hold back whatever it was that had turned them that colour. He looked…he looked like a man filled with suppressed anger, Charley recognised. And as he came towards her he was looking at her as though she was the source and the cause of that anger.

'What is it?' she asked apprehensively.

'What is it? It's *this*,' Raphael answered savagely, reaching for her, pulling her against his body and then bending his head to kiss her. Not as he had kissed her before, not as she had dreamed of him kissing her, but over and over again, as though he couldn't stop. Fierce, hard, demanding kisses, filled with a raw and angry pent-up passion that seared through her, igniting inside her an answering, equally primitive need.

Charley lost all sense of time as she clung to him, riding out the storm, letting him take what he wanted, glorying in the hard, imprisoning hold of his hands on her body that made her his willing captive. But at last she somehow managed to pull herself away from him to warn him, 'Anna will be bringing my supper.'

'Not now,' he told her, pulling her back towards him, his hand finding her bare thigh beneath her towel and caressing it, making her quiver with a thrill of yearning pleasure. 'I told Anna we are not to be disturbed. Your hunger for your supper will, I am afraid, have to go unsatisfied, because my hunger for you cannot bear any further delay.'

His hand had reached the top of her thigh; his voice was thick with emotion. Her heart was pounding with wild, out-of-control euphoria. He wanted her. Raphael wanted her.

Charlotte pressed herself closer to him in eager delight, another thrill running through her when he groaned and kissed her fiercely, the open agony of his longing matching everything that she herself felt.

Their mutual need was like a fireball, consuming them. Raphael was shedding his clothes as he caressed her with increasing urgency and intimacy. There was no time for the slow sensuality of leisurely love play, and no need either, Charley acknowledged. How could there be when she had spent the last three weeks aching for him? An ache that had become a tumultuous clamour of pulsing need, possessing the whole of her body even before she had seen how his hunger for her had brought Raphael to full and thick readiness. It was the sight of that readiness that sent her over the edge and into a place of wild, visceral need.

She could see the hot look of male urgency glittering in Raphael's eyes as he parted her naked thighs, the heat of his hand against her sex making her moan. The sound changed to a fevered gasp of almost too heightened pleasure when his fingers stroked the eager waiting length of her sex.

'I've lain awake night after night thinking of you like this—sweet and hot, wet and ready for me.'

Just the sound of his voice was enough to make her body convulse with longing.

There was no time for them to reach the bed—no thought in her head other than the need to have Raphael deep within her, filling her, completing her, driving her with each wonderfully powerful thrust of his body closer to the epicentre of the storm within her... Her legs wrapped around Raphael, her fingernails digging deep into his shoulders. His hands protected her back from the hardness of the bedroom door as they coupled wildly and

fiercely. Charley could feel her body's pos-
sessive hunger for him as her muscles tightened around him, demanding that he take her
deeper, harder, faster. Words formed by her
aching need were gasped against his shoulder,
his sweat-dampened throat. She could smell
the aroused heat of his body, taste his need in
the salty tang of his skin.

The end came quickly and almost violently,
in a series of frantic mini-orgasms for Charley
that built in intensity until Raphael tensed and
made an agonised sound of release against her
skin, his completion within her inciting a final
orgasm that took her to new heights and held
her there, whilst her body convulsed on wave
after wave of pleasure.

Drained and trembling, Charley unwrapped
her legs from Raphael's body, too weak to
stand unsupported on her own, simply
leaning into him as he held her, their hearts
pounding together in the aftermath of what
they had shared.

* * *

They had eaten, showered, made love again— this time with Raphael slowly building her desire with sensuality and an awareness of her needs that had brought tears of emotion to her eyes.

'Stay with me,' Charley whispered as Raphael held her protectively in the curve of his body, and they both knew that it wasn't just for tonight that she wanted him to stay.

CHAPTER THIRTEEN

A SHADOW blotted out the morning sunlight warming her face, causing Charley to murmur a protest in her sleep. Just as she had done earlier, when he'd eased her out of his arms so that he could shower and dress, Raphael noted. The morning light fell harshly against the planes of his face, revealing a certain gauntness and weariness of spirit. He shouldn't have come here last night—shouldn't have left the safety of Rome even though it had become an imprisoning barren waste of aching. He had no right to take what he had given his vow to himself not to.

The temptation to simply walk away whilst Charlotte slept was almost overwhelming, but he made himself overcome it, leaning down to place his hand on her body—not on her bare rounded shoulder; he was far too raw to be able to trust himself to touch her skin to skin. Instead he placed his hand gently on the spot where her arm lay beneath the bedclothes.

Charley woke up immediately, her sleepy gaze sharpening into focus, delight brimming in it as she sat up, exclaiming, 'Raphael!'

Everything about her demeanour spoke openly and joyously of her feelings. Raphael could see her love for him in the way she smiled at him, hear it in the upward lilt of her voice, feel it in the softly sensuous yearning movement of her body towards him.

He drew in a sharp breath and stepped back from the bed, turning away from her to look towards the window as he told her, 'I shall be returning to Rome in half an hour, but first I need to talk to you about last night.'

Charley felt the weight of his words as though they were the onset of an avalanche that was going to crush the life out of her. In the short space of time it took Raphael to say them, the happiness with which she had awoken had turned to fear.

'Last night?' she repeated.

Raphael nodded his head.

'Last night should never have happened. The blame for the fact that it did lies entirely with me. I should have had more self-control; I should not have come here and given in to my...need. It mustn't happen again. It will not happen again.'

Charley couldn't hide her distressed anguish.

'I don't understand,' she protested. 'You want me, and I want you.'

'Yes.'

Raphael's voice was terse. He wasn't looking at her, and Charley could see the way his jaw tensed.

'Then why can't we be together? I love you, Raphael.'

'Yes, I know, and that is part of the reason why it must end. I cannot give you... There is no future for us. It is better, kinder, fairer to you, that we end things now.'

No future for them? Pain and anger filled Charley.

'Why is there no future for us? Because I'm not good enough for you, The Duke? Is that why you said what you did about me not conceiving your child? I'm not good enough to be the mother of a baby with your precious blue blood, is that it?'

She was working herself up into a fury because it was the only way she had of stopping herself from begging him to change his mind. She had to hold on to her anger because it was all she had to cling to.

'No. Never that.' Raphael swung round as he uttered the tormented denial, the sunlight revealing the new thinness of his face, his expression that of a man emotionally tortured beyond his own bearing.

'Tell me what it is, then,' Charley insisted. '*Tell* me.'

She could see his chest expanding as he took a deep, ragged breath.

'Very well, then. You saw for yourself how

I reacted last night—how my anger over-whelmed me, how I took hold of you in anger and violence.'

'Because you were afraid that the car would hit me.'

'I wish I could believe it was only that that motivated me, but I cannot let myself accept that. Last night I broke every vow I have ever made to myself. It must never happen again. I am not saying that things must end between us because I do not want you to have my child, but because I will not put you in a position where I might hurt you. Just as I will not pass on to any child the poisoned inheritance that is in my own genes.'

Whilst Charley looked at him in shocked bewilderment, Raphael loosened the tension out of his shoulders with a tired movement.

'You will want to know what I mean?'

'Yes,' Charley agreed.

'It is a long story—as long as the history of my mother's family. She was descended from the bloodline of one of the most bloodthirsty of all the Beccelli family. During the fifteenth century his cruelty and sadism was such that it was expunged from all family documents. His greed knew no bounds. In order to empower himself he waged war on his neighbours, amongst them my mother's family, giving orders that the sons of the family should be killed along with their parents, whilst taking for himself their daughter to be married to one of his own sons—but not before he had raped her and impregnated her.'

Raphael heard Charley's indrawn gasp.

'His cruelty was unimaginable—the product of a twisted and sadistic mind. Finally he was brought to rough justice when he was murdered by his own sons, who then fell out amongst themselves, killing one another and leaving behind them the young raped bride who was carrying the child of her abuser. From that time down through my mother's family there have been those who have manifested sadism—men and women who have carried out acts of unspeakable cruelty. My mother's own great-grandfather was one of those people, as was a male cousin—who ended up being murdered in a brothel. There were other members of her family—less openly affected but possessed of terrible tempers, given to uncontrollable rages. Because of her dread of passing on the curse of that inheritance my mother had sworn never to marry or have a child, so that no future generations would be contaminated by her inheritance. But then she met my father. They were passionately in love with one another, and he persuaded her to marry him. She told me over and over again during my childhood how she had promised herself that she would not burden future generations with the burden she herself had had to carry, how madness brought on by guilt as well as sadism destroyed the lives of so many who shared her blood.'

Charley had to swallow hard before she could speak. Raphael's revelations had filled her with pity for him, and a fiercely protective love.

'But you are neither of those things,' was all she felt able to say. 'You are no sadist, Raphael, and you are not mad.'

'Not yet—although that is not to say that I will never be, nor that my child will not be.'

It took several seconds for the full horror of what he was saying to sink into Charley's mind.

'But you can't know that it will happen,' she managed.

'No. But, far more importantly I cannot know that it will not—and because of that I cannot take the risk, not for you and not for a child. Even if it is free of the taint of our shared blood, he or she in turn will have to carry the burden that will be born with them, and they will have to make the decision that I was not strong enough to make for them. It is my belief that in speaking to me as she did my mother was asking me to do what she had not been able to do.'

'But you are a duke, and without an heir…'

'I have an heir—the son of a cousin who is my closest male relative on my father's

side, and so untainted.' Raphael dismissed
Charley's statement. 'The reason I am telling
you this is not because I want your pity but
because I want you to understand why we
cannot be together. Already you have witnessed my anger—how are we to know how
that darkness within me might grow?'

'That was a completely natural reaction,
and my fault.'

'No, last night is not the first time such a rage
has possessed me. After my mother's death I
went into her sitting room—the room she
always loved best. I could almost see her
sitting there in her favourite chair, but she
wasn't there, and because of that I destroyed
that chair by smashing it against the fireplace.'

'You were just a boy,' Charley protested. 'A
boy who had lost both his parents and who was
alone and frightened.'

Raphael turned to her, giving her a tormented look of mingled desire and denial.

'Do you not think I would like to tell myself
that? That I would like to believe it? But I cannot.

I must not. Because it may not be the truth, and because there is no way of knowing whether or not I possess my mother's family's curse.'

'I love you, Raphael, and I am willing to take the risk.'

'Maybe so, but I am not.'

'Because you don't love me?' Charley challenged him. Surely if she could get him to say that he loved her then she would be able to find a way to persuade him to let her share his life?

'No, I don't love you.'

The pain that seized her was crucifying, unbearable. Without knowing it she made a small sound, agonised and heartrending. Raphael closed his eyes. He must not weaken. It was for her sake that he was denying her—for her future.

'Don't you think if I *did* love you that I would still say there could be nothing between us? Don't you think that if I loved you my concern would be for you, for your ultimate happiness, your right to love a man you will never need to fear—a man who can give you the child or children that you will also love.'

His voice became harsher as he told her, 'I cannot and will not imprison you in a relationship which ultimately you will come to resent. I can't. I have told you that, and if there were by some mischance to be a child...' He paused and then told her heavily, 'It is my belief that my mother took her own life after my father's death, because she was afraid of being alone with the responsibility of what she might have passed on to me and through me to generations as yet unborn.'

Charley's heart ached with compassion and love.

'I refuse to believe that you are affected by your family's affliction, Raphael, and as for children—for a woman who loves you, who truly loves you as I do, you yourself would be enough,' she told him fiercely, unable to keep her emotions out of her voice.

Now, at last, he turned fully to look at her. The morning sunlight was cruel, revealing the toll his openness with her had taken on his haunted features.

'You cannot know that I will not be affected. Neither of us can. Do you think I want to see you recoil from me in horror and fear? To see the love shining in your eyes now turn to horror?'

Charley desperately wanted to go to him and hold him, almost as a mother might hold her child. He was the man she loved and he always would be. What he had revealed to her had only made her love him more, not less, just as it had made her want to share with him his exile from what other people took for granted.

'Raphael, please let me share this with you,' she begged him.

'No,' Raphael answered. 'To love someone and not yearn to create with them the miracle of a new life from that love is an act of denial beyond the limits of my own control. I may not have known that before, but I know it now. I learned that when I held you in my arms. I will not allow what I feel for you to chain you to me. Love—true, real love—has to be stronger than that. It must put what is right for the person loved above its own needs and desires.'

Raphael was saying that he loved her?

Joy lifted her heart—only for it to crash down again as she took in the full meaning of what Raphael had said.

'You cannot make that decision for me,' she told him. 'If you love me then—'

'Then nothing.' Raphael stopped her, his voice harsh. 'I cannot offer you my love and still think of myself as a man of honour. You must see that?'

'What I see,' Charley told him spiritedly, 'is that you are making us both suffer when we don't have to over an issue that may not even exist. I love you, Raphael. Of course I would love to have your child—but I will gladly and willingly sacrifice doing so to be with you and share your life.'

'I cannot allow you to do that.' His mouth twisted—the mouth she had kissed so passionately last night—and the lips that had touched her body so intimately, bringing her such pleasure, now held a cynical twist, causing her intense pain.

'Your own choice of words reveals the truth—you describe not having a child as a sacrifice,' Raphael told her. 'You cannot deny it. You used that description of your own volition.'

Charley could see that it was pointless for her to wish the word unsaid. She raged inwardly, blaming herself for her thoughtlessness, thinking how bitterly unfair it was that the whole of her future happiness should hang on one simple word.

'You may love me now, Charlotte,' Raphael told her, 'but there will come a time when the ache inside you for a child will be stronger than the ache inside you for me. I cannot let that happen. Not for my sake, but for yours. I am already guilty of allowing my own selfish need to overcome my principles, and in doing so I am hurting you. I shall not do so any more. When I return to Rome I will speak to my lawyer and to your employer, to arrange for someone else to take your place here, working on the project.'

Raphael ignored Charlotte's stifled protest.

'I shall, of course, compensate you financially…' he continued.

'Pay me off, you mean? Like a discarded toy you don't want any more? Is that how you always treat the women you sleep with, Raphael—by paying them off once you have had what you wanted from them?'

White-faced with grief, Charley flung the words at him, retreating to the top of the bed when he strode towards her, to grasp her shoulders and almost shake her.

'You will not say that,' he told her. 'You will not demean what we shared together and yourself by speaking in such a way. The money has nothing to do with our personal relationship. It is to compensate you because you will be losing your job.'

It was because his emotions were so raw that he was angry with her, Charley knew. The thought crossed her mind that if she increased that anger, if she really, really pushed him, then that emotion might spill over into a passion that would result in them making love, giving her a chance to prove to him that what they felt for one another was too strong to be ignored. Shame flooded through her. She must not taint what they had shared last night by attempting to manipulate him. She did not want her memories soured by her own shame.

Raphael released her, stepping back from her, removing the temptation to ignore her better self.

'It will take some time for everything to be sorted out—a couple of weeks at least, I imagine—and during that time it will be necessary for you to remain here at the *palazzo*.'

'And where will you be?' Charley had to ask him.

'I shall be in Rome. I cannot be here,' Raphael told her bleakly. 'Not now. It would be too much—for both of us. Do not look at me like that,' he warned her. 'I am doing this for your sake, and one day you will thank me for it.'

Charley shook her head, her vision of him blurred by the tears filling her eyes.

'No,' she told him brokenly. 'I will never do that, and I will never stop loving you.'

He was walking towards the door. She couldn't let him go.

'Raphael, please,' she begged him, running towards him, the sunlight splashing her naked body with golden light.

He had reached the door.

She put her hands on his arms and pleaded, 'We could be together. I understand now why the garden and its restoration is so important to you. It's because it is what you will give to posterity, isn't it? Instead of your children— your son. We could do it together, Raphael; together we could restore and create something of great beauty to give to your people.'

Charley felt the shudder that ripped through his body.

'Trust a woman to find some ridiculous and fictitious emotional fairytale and insist on substituting it for reason,' said Raphael, dismissing her statement, but he knew that she had touched a nerve. Her words were like the careful, gentle touch of an archaeologist, brushing away a protective covering to reveal something unbearably fragile beneath it. Only in his case what she had revealed was not some priceless piece of antiquity but instead his pitiful attempt to find a substitute in his life for all that he could not have—to find a purpose and a meaning that would compensate him for what he had to deny himself.

Charley's naked body was pressed close to his own, her face turned up to his, her gaze brimming with love and hope. All he had to do was open his arms to her and she would be his for ever. There would be no turning back. He would have her love to sustain him through the darkest of dark nights.

'A garden lives and breathes, Raphael, it gives love and joy to those who come into it. We could share that. It could be ours…'

The pain was almost too much for him. It reached out to every single part of him, along with the awareness of all that would be lost to him. He had to resist temptation. He had to endure the pain—for Charley. Desperately, Raphael formed a mental image of Charley—

not as she was now, but as she would be holding her child in her arms, her whole body alight with the love she felt for it. Her child, but never, ever his.

'No!' he told her harshly, reaching for the door handle, forcing her to release him and step back from him.

It was over. There could be no going back.

CHAPTER FOURTEEN

SHE would be leaving Florence in ten days'
time. Everything was arranged. She had her
ticket; she would be picked up and driven to
the airport—all she had to do was ensure that
her paperwork was left in order and her ap-
pointments cancelled.

Charley started to pull open the drawer in
the desk, to remove the desk diary she kept as
an extra back-up reminder of the appoint-
ments stored electronically, determined to
make sure that professionally nothing was
overlooked. Her misery overflowed into irritation when the drawer wouldn't open
properly. Kneeling down in front of the desk,
she felt inside the drawer, quickly realising

that the diary had become wedged against the underside of the desk. Picking up her ruler, she used it to try and prise the diary free, exhaling in impatient relief when she finally succeeded. The force of her probing, though, had sent the diary skidding right to the back of the drawer, with a definite thud of sound, obliging her to pull the drawer further out. Only when she did so, to her dismay, there was no sign of the diary and the back of the drawer itself was missing.

She had damaged Raphael's mother's desk. Horrified, Charley pulled the drawer out completely, and then frowned as she realised how much shorter it was than the full depth of the desk. Very carefully she slid her hand and her arm into the empty space where the drawer had been, feeling her way to the back of the space. It was more or less the same depth as the drawer, and indeed a good ten inches short of the depth of the desk. Curious now, Charley re-examined the space, pressing against the back wall and then exhaling in triumph when it suddenly gave way. It must be a hidden compartment, operated by a spring, and she must have inadvertently touched it when she had pushed her diary free. It was too deep for her to reach inside it, so she had to use her ruler again to edge out her diary and bring it within her reach. Only it wasn't just the diary she had edged out. There was something else as well: several thick sheets of expensive notepaper, poking out of an envelope that had obviously never been sealed.

Uncertainly Charley turned the envelope over, her heartbeat accelerating as she stared at what was written on it.

To my beloved son, Raphael…

Charley sank down onto the floor, still holding the envelope, her diary forgotten.

This was a letter to Raphael from his mother. It had to be. And she had no right to read it, but her hand was trembling so much that somehow the letter had begun to slip free of the envelope, the thick sheets sliding into her lap.

Putting down the envelope, Charley quickly picked the paper up.

Impossible now not to be aware of the elegant handwriting, of the date written at the top of the first sheet in dark ink.

The letter was nearly twenty years old, written quite obviously when Raphael had only been a boy. An aching longing filled her, a tender smile for the boy that Raphael must have been curving her mouth.

She looked down at the letter, the words written on it springing up as though demanding that she read them.

My dearest and dearly loved son—and you are that, Raphael, MY son, the son of my heart and my love. I am writing this letter to you in English because it is the language that my English governess taught me, as your father and I have taught it to you, so that we could all speak it to-

gether—our special 'secret' shared language. Your father is gone now, and my life without him is so empty. One day, when you yourself know true love, you will understand all that this means.

I write this letter now, knowing that it is what your father would want me to do. It is to be given to you when you come of age. We had planned to tell you together, and I fear I shall not have the strength to tell you on my own.

I beg you not to judge me too harshly, Raphael, for being too cowardly, too afraid of losing your love, to tell you the truth myself. The truth, though, must be told—for your own dear sake.

Now you are young, a boy still, but one day you will be a man, and when that time comes there are things that you will need to know.

She mustn't read any more, Charley told herself. She must fold up the letter and hand it to Anna to send on to Raphael. To continue to read something so obviously private was a gross invasion of the privacy of mother and son. And yet she was filled with a compulsion that she could not resist to read on.

Spreading out the heavy sheets of paper, Charley continued to read.

You know already of the terrible inheritance that has come down to me through my family. I have told you stories of lives ruined and destroyed, of the horror of the cruelty and madness that has surfaced in members of our blood, and part of the reason I have told you this is so that you will understand why your father and I chose to do what we have done.

You are my beloved son, Raphael, the greatest gift life has given me along with the love of your father. From the first moment of your conception, even before I held you in my arms for the first time, I loved you. You are my son, my child, even though the source that gave you life was not me.

I made a vow as a girl that I would not pass on to a child the burden that I had had to carry—the knowledge that whilst I had escaped the taint of our blood, my children, and their children after them might not do so. When your father and I married he knew of this vow I had made and he supported me in it. However, as the years went by I yearned increasingly to hold a child of our love in my arms. That need became a sickness in me for which I believed there could be no cure, until I learned that there was a doctor—not here in Italy but abroad—who had discovered a way to enable women who could not conceive naturally to have a child of their own. Initially your father was against such a thing, but he knew of my desperation, and so in the end he gave way, and we travelled abroad to see this doctor. He warned us that it would not be easy, nor the result guaranteed, but now I had hope—the hope of having a child from the love your father and I shared that would be free of my own blood.

So it was that your life began, with the gift of life from a childhood friend of mine of good family who had fallen on hard times. A woman with children of her own, who understood my need.

Those first early weeks when I knew that I carried you inside my body I hardly dared to believe that you actually were there. I was so afraid that I might lose you, but you yourself gave me strength, Raphael, because you were there, growing. You had not rejected me or spurned my body; instead you had made yourself part of me. I cannot tell you the joy I felt because you had accepted me as your mother, because you trusted me to protect you and provide for you. With every day that went by my strength grew because of your strength. I was so proud of you, so proud to be carrying you, your father's child, growing within me. Even before you were born I knew you and loved you.

To me you were mine every bit as much as you would have been had you been conceived from me. When after your birth you were placed in my arms I was joyful—not just because you were the image of your father, or even because I was holding you, but because I knew your life would be free of the shadows of my family past.

Over the years I have told you over and over again about that past, hoping that when the time came for me to tell you what I have written here you would understand and not turn away from me, or accuse me of deceit, no longer thinking of me as your mother. Even if you should do that, Raphael, you will always be my child, my so beloved son, who I carried with such joy and pride and who I have watched grow with equal joy and pride.

Charley lifted her head from the letter, biting her lip in an attempt to stem the tears spilling from her eyes. Every word she had written was filled with Raphael's mother's love for him, and reading the letter Charley had felt her emotion.

Why, though, had she hidden the letter away? There was no signature to it. Perhaps she had put it aside to be finished at a later date, but had not had the opportunity to do so?

How selfless a mother's love could be. Raphael's mother's desire to ensure that her son need not fear her past had come before her own obvious fear that the truth might come between them.

The truth!

Charley sat back on her heels. She was only just beginning to appreciate herself what the letter would mean—not only for Raphael himself, but also for them!

They could be together. Now there was nothing to keep them apart. Now they could love one another, without Raphael feeling that he was denying her anything.

She wanted to jump up and dance around the room. She was filled with energy and impatience. She would drive to Rome, take the letter herself to Raphael, so that she could be there when he read it. She knew that he would not reject his mother, that like her he would know how much and how selflessly she had loved him as her own child.

Her mind was racing ahead, making plans, but then abruptly a new thought struck her.

What if she was taking too much for granted? Raphael was a duke, the holder of an ancient title and estate, a member of a group of people who tended to marry within their own class in order to produce heirs. Raphael might have seemed to care about her when he had believed that he must never have children, but what if his mother's revelations changed that? Just as he had put his concern for her future before his own feelings, wasn't it only right and fair that she should step back a bit now and allow him to come to her freely?

And if he didn't? If he should turn away from her? Charley shuddered under the misery of the pain that bit deeply into her. She had to do what was right—for Raphael.

An hour later she stood and watched as the courier drove away from the *palazzo,* taking with him the letter she had written to Raphael, enclosing his mother's letter to him, to be delivered by special delivery, no later than the morning.

She had been open and honest with him in her letter, admitting to reading what his mother had written, telling him how much she loved him and saying she hoped that now they could be together, but telling him as well that she would wait for him to make contact with her, and if he did not then she would leave for England, as arranged, and accept that their relationship was over.

She told herself she was worrying unnecessarily, because Raphael *did* love her. He had told her so himself. He had said, too, how much he wanted her as the mother of his children. It was foolish of her to have any doubts, but it was the right thing to do to wait for him to come to her to confirm his feelings for her.

By this time tomorrow he would be here, and she would be in his arms.

CHAPTER FIFTEEN

IT WAS over, Charley acknowledged bleakly, as the plane taking her home to Manchester began its descent through the grey clouds to the rain-soaked tarmac of the airport. Her throat felt raw from the tears she refused to allow herself to cry. Now, with them threatening again, she had to close her eyes tightly, no doubt making the man sitting next to her think she was a nervous passenger. Charley smiled wryly.

Right up until the last moment she had gone on hoping—right up until the car had arrived for her this morning and she had finally had to accept that Raphael did not want her.

It was ten days now since she had sent him

the letters. At first with every new hour she had expected to see him arrive at the *palazzo*, to take her in his arms and tell her how much he loved her.

But when the hours and then the days began to pass, without him making any contact with her at all, her expectation had turned to despair. Unable to eat or sleep, she had watched hollow-eyed, night after night, unable to sleep, simply staring out through her bedroom window into the darkness, hoping against hope that he would appear.

His silence meant that her pride would not allow her to contact him again—not so much as an e-mail. What was the point when he had made it so very clear that he no longer wanted her?

Soon now she would be home. Home? There was no home for her now. It was hard for her to keep her misery at bay as the plane touched down. Her only true home, the only home she wanted, was within Raphael's heart, and there was no place there for her. She was an outcast, denied the only place she wanted to be, the only man she wanted to love.

The arrivals hall was busy with people pressing close to the barriers, eager to see the friends and family they were there to welcome. Charley barely spared them a glance. She hadn't warned her own family to expect her, clinging on right to the last second before her plane took off to the hope that by some miracle Raphael would not allow her to leave.

How foolish she had been—but at least she had her memories. She was past the waiting crowd now and in the arrivals hall proper, thronged with tired travellers intent on making their way to whatever transport they had arranged to get them from the airport to their homes. She would have to take a taxi—expensive, but fortunately the house she shared with her sisters in South Manchester wasn't very far from the airport.

She could hear the sound of movement behind her—someone walking fast, someone reaching for her arm. No, not someone, she recognised weakly as she turned round. Not someone at all, but the only one.

'Raphael...' As she breathed his name Charley wondered if somehow he was merely a figment of her imagination, an image she had conjured up out of her own need—because how could he be here?

But he was, and he was pulling her into his arms and holding her there, his heart thumping heavily and fast against her.

'I can't believe you're here,' was all Charley could manage to say.

'Believe it,' Raphael responded. 'Believe it, and believe too that I will not leave your side until you have promised that you will never leave me again.'

'I thought it was what you wanted,' Charley tried to protest, but her heart wasn't in it—it was far too busy racing with joy and disbelief because Raphael was here, with her.

'You are what I want—all I want—all I will ever want. I can't go on without you. I thought

I could, but I can't. Will you marry me, Charlotte Wareham? Will you come back to Italy with me and be my wife?'

He looked and sounded so humble, or at least as humble as it was possible for such a naturally proud man to be, that Charley suspected she would have forgiven him anything.

'There is nothing I want more than for us to be together, Raphael.'

'We will be married as soon as it can be arranged. I do not intend to risk losing you again.' He was holding her hand now, twining his fingers through her own, lacing the two of them together.

'I have been thinking about this matter of children,' he told her abruptly. He was looking at a point over her shoulder, and his jaw was tensing, Charley observed, as it did when he was trying to control his emotions.

'With modern-day medical science it is perfectly possible for us to have a child that will not carry my genes—a child, that will be born of you but will not carry my genes. A child that

I will love as my own because it is part of you. That way I shall not be depriving you of motherhood. And, as for myself, if the day should come when it becomes evident that I have inherited my mother's family's curse then I shall end our marriage and give you your freedom.'

Charley stared at him in confused bewilderment, unable to say anything as the thoughts rushed around inside her head. Hadn't he read her letter?

'Did you get the letter I sent to you in Rome?' she asked him.

Immediately Raphael frowned.

'No. I left Rome three days after we parted. I could not work, I could not sleep—I could not do anything but think about you and all that I had lost. I own a small skiing chalet up in the mountains. I went there, intending to force myself to give up all thoughts of you, but instead I came to realise that I could not bear my life without you. I began to think that maybe you were right—that maybe my anger was not a sign of what I had inherited. I wanted to believe that more than you can know, because it was my way back to you. Then I told myself that we could still have a child—a child that would carry your genes only—and my hopes grew. All I wanted was to be with you, to talk with you and ask you to be my wife, but there was an accident on my way back to Rome.'

'An accident?' Anxiety sharpened Charley's voice. 'What happened? Are you all right?'

'It was my own fault. I was driving too fast, concentrating on being with you instead of on my driving. Luckily no damage was done other than to the Ferrari, but the hospital insisted on keeping me overnight in case I had concussion, even though I told them that it was vitally important that I be allowed to leave. Unfortunately I was too late. As I arrived at the airport your plane was taking off.'

'But you got here before me. How…?'

'I hired a private plane,' Raphael told her dismissively.

'Oh, Raphael.' Charley blinked back her tears. 'Are you sure about what you're saying? About us being together and everything?'

He didn't flinch.

'I mean every word I have said to you. I love you more than I ever thought it possible for me to love anyone. You are my life, my heartbeat, every breath in my body. You are everything to me, Charlotte, and without you I am nothing—there is nothing. Say you will marry me. Come home with me. Tell me that you love me.'

'I do love you, Raphael,' Charley confirmed, 'but there is something I have to tell you before we can talk about marriage— something important.'

She could see that he was concerned, even though he tried to conceal it from her.

'Very well, but we will discuss this oh, so important matter in the comfort of the plane and not here.'

That would mean going back to Italy with him, and if, once he knew the truth about his own birth, he should change his mind about wanting to marry her she would have to leave all over again. But how could she deny him what he was asking after what he had told her?

Unable to trust herself to speak, silently Charley nodded her head.

CHAPTER SIXTEEN

THE plane had taken off. They were alone in the comfort of its elegant interior, furnished more like a small sitting room than any kind of aircraft with which Charley was familiar.

The minute the steward had left them Raphael had taken her in his arms, kissing her so passionately and with such longing that Charley had been incapable of doing anything other than responding.

'I cannot wait for us to be alone,' Raphael told her. 'I cannot wait to make you properly mine again, to hold you in my arms and love you. We will spend tonight in Florence, at the apartment, and then tomorrow we will start to make the arrangements for our marriage.'

What if she simply didn't tell him? What if she begged him to stay with her until after they were married and he didn't see the letter until it was too late and he was committed to her? He had, after all, said that he loved her. Why should she risk losing him when she loved him so much?

Charley closed her eyes, willing away the temptation tormenting her.

'There is something you have to know… something you *must* know, just in case you should want to change your mind about marrying me.'

There—she had said it, and now Raphael was looking at her with that same haughty frown she remembered from the first time she had seen him.

'So what is this something—this secret from your past?'

'It isn't from my past, Raphael. It's from yours.'

Hardly daring to risk looking at him, in case she lost her courage, Charley plunged on.

'Whilst I was clearing my things from your

mother's desk, by accident I found a concealed compartment. There was a letter in it. A letter your mother had written to you and for you. I shouldn't have read it, but I did…I sent it to you in Rome by special delivery. I hoped that when you'd read it you'd come to me, and when you didn't I assumed…that is to say…'

'A letter from my mother? How can that affect our plans to marry?'

Charley took a deep breath.

'Raphael, although you didn't know it when you made that suggestion, that selfless suggestion about us having a child, you were following in your own mother's footsteps. She loved you so much—so very, very much—her love for you shines out of her letter. Reading it made me cry. She carried you in her body, Raphael, she loved you as her child, but you were not her biological child. Like you, she did not want to take the risk of burdening a child with her own inheritance, and like you she made the decision to allow medical science to provide her with the means of giving birth to your father's child without that child having to carry her genes. The reason she told you so often about those genes was because she hoped that when you knew the truth you would understand that she had taken the steps she did take to protect you—because her love for you was such that she wanted you to be free of fear, for yourself and your descendants.'

Raphael's face was drained of colour and his mouth was set grimly. Charley's heart sank. Surely he was not going to reject his mother's love for him?

'And because of this you have doubts about marrying me?'

Charley was astounded.

'No, of course not. There is nothing I want more than to marry you. It is for *your* sake that I wanted you to know. Don't you see, Raphael? Your mother's letter changes everything. Now you are free to marry and have children, to have an heir, you can marry anyone you wish—someone far more suitable to be the mother of your son than I am.'

'More suitable? How could that be possible? There is no one more suitable to bear my children than you. How could there be when it is you that I love?'

'Oh, Raphael.'

She was in his arms, holding him as tightly as he was holding her, kissing him as passionately and hungrily as he was kissing her.

'You are my life,' he told her fiercely. 'My love and my life.'

They kissed again, sweetly and tenderly this time, their kiss a shared vow, a shared commitment to their love and their future together.

'When the garden is finished, could we name it for your mother, do you think?' Charley asked Raphael as he released her.

She could see the sheen of emotion in his eyes when he looked down at her.

'Yes,' he told her. 'We will name it for her in remembrance of the gift of love she gave to me when she gave me life.'

'How long do you think it will be before we are in Florence?' Charley whispered against his lips as she kissed him again.

'Far too long for the way I feel at the moment,' Raphael answered. 'Far far too long.'

Only it wasn't, and by the time the sun was setting they were standing together in the privacy of the bedroom where Raphael had first made love to her. The scent that was the only covering Charley was wearing filled the evening air.

'This was what I wanted when you gave it to me,' Charley told Raphael. 'I wanted to lie in your arms wearing only the scent and your touch.'

A delicate quiver of erotic pleasure ran through her when Raphael gathered her naked body against his own, and her love for him filled her when he told her huskily, 'I love you more than I can find the words to say. You have made me complete and brought light to the darkest places of my life. Now that you are mine I shall never let you go.'

'And I shall never want you to,' Charley promised him.

Mills & Boon® Online

Discover more romance at
www.millsandboon.co.uk

- 🌹 **FREE** online reads
- 🌹 **Books** up to one month before shops
- 🌹 **Browse our books** before you buy

...and much more!

For exclusive competitions and instant updates:

 Like us on **facebook.com/romancehq**

 Follow us on **twitter.com/millsandboonuk**

 Join us on **community.millsandboon.co.uk**

Visit us Online | Sign up for our FREE eNewsletter at **www.millsandboon.co.uk**